Azalea:
Temperance

Temperance was probably
Keane Prescott's middle name!
Jovilette Wilder's new boss
was too cool and controlled, but
then he surprised her with a
long, lingering kiss that was
anything but calm!

NORA ROBERTS
LANGUAGE OF LOVE

Love has a language all its own, and for
centuries, flowers have symbolized
love's finest expression.
Discover the language of flowers
—and love—
in this romantic collection of 48 favorite
books by bestselling author Nora Roberts.

NORA ROBERTS

LANGUAGE OF LOVE

UNTAMED

Silhouette Books

For my sons,
Life's a circus.
Go for it!

SILHOUETTE BOOKS
300 East 42nd St., New York, N.Y. 10017

UNTAMED © 1983 by Nora Roberts.
First published as a Silhouette Romance.

Language of Love edition published October 1991.

ISBN: 0-373-51028-4

Printed in U.S.A.

Chapter One

At the crack of the whip, twelve lions stood on their haunches and pawed the air. On command, they began to leap from pedestal to pedestal in a quick, close-formation, figure-eight pattern. This required split-second timing. With voice and hand commands the trainer kept the tawny, springing bodies moving.

"Well done, Pandora."

At her name and the signal, the muscular lioness leaped to the ground and lay down on her side. One by one the others followed suit, until, snarling and baring their teeth, they stretched across the tanbark. A male was positioned beside each female; at a sharp reproof from the trainer, Merlin ceased nibbling on Ophelia's ear.

"Heads up!" They obeyed as the trainer walked briskly in front of them. The whip was tossed aside with a flourish, then, with apparent nonchalance, the trainer reclined lengthwise across the warm bodies. The center cat, a full-maned African, let out a great, echoing bellow. As a reward for his response to the cue, his ear was given a good scratching. The trainer rose from the feline couch, clapped hands and brought the lions to their feet. Then, with a hand signal, each was called by name and sent through the chute and into their cages. One stayed behind, a huge, black-maned cat who, like an ordinary tabby, circled and rubbed up against his trainer's legs.

Deftly, a rope was attached to a chain that was hidden under his mane. Then, with swift agility, the trainer mounted the lion's back. As the door of the big cage opened, lion and rider passed through for a tour of the practice ring. When they reached the back door of the ring barn, Merlin, the obliging lion, was transferred to a wheel cage.

"Well, Duffy." Jo turned after the cage was secured. "Are we ready for the road?"

Duffy was a small, round man with a monk's fringe of chestnut hair and a face that exploded with ginger freckles. His open smile and Irish blue eyes gave him the look of an aging choirboy. His mind was sharp, shrewd and scrappy. He was the best manager Prescott's Circus Colossus could have had.

"Since we open in Ocala tomorrow," he replied in a raspy voice, "you'd better be ready." He shifted his fat cigar stump from the right side of his mouth to the left.

Jo merely smiled, then stretched to loosen muscles grown taut during the thirty minutes in the cage. "My cats are ready, Duffy. It's been a long winter. They need to get back on the road as much as the rest of us."

Duffy frowned. As circumstances had it, he
stood only inches higher than his animal trainer.
Widely spaced, almond-shaped eyes stared back
at him. They were as sharp and green as emer-
alds, surrounded by thick, inky lashes. At the
moment they were fearless and amused, but
Duffy had seen them frightened, vulnerable and
lost. He shifted his cigar again and took two
quick puffs as Jo gave a cage hand instructions.

He remembered Steve Wilder, Jo's father. He
had been one of the best cat men in the business.
Jo was as good with the cats as Wilder had been.
In some ways, Duffy acknowledged, even better.
But she had the traits of her mother: delicate
build; dark, passionate looks. Jolivette Wilder
was as slender as her aerialist mother had been,
with bold green eyes and straight, raven black
hair that fell to just below her waist. Her brows
were delicately arched, her nose small and
straight, her cheekbones high and elegant, while
her mouth was full and soft. Her skin was tawny
from the Florida sun; it added to her gypsy-like
appearance. Confidence added spark to the
beauty.

Finishing her instructions, Jo tucked her arm
through Duffy's. She had seen that frown before. "Somebody quit?" she asked as they began to walk toward Duffy's office.

"Nope."

His monosyllabic reply caused Jo to lift a
brow. It was not often Duffy answered any ques-

tion briefly. Years of experience told her to hold her tongue as they moved across the compound.

Rehearsals were going on everywhere. Vito the wire walker informally sharpened his act on a cable stretched between two trees. The Mendalsons called out to each other as they tossed their juggling pins high in the air, while the equestrian act led their horses into the ring barn. She saw one of the Stevenson girls walking on stilts. She'd be six now, Jo mused, tossing the hair from her eyes as she watched the young girl's wavering progress. Jo remembered the year she had been born. It had been that same year that she had been allowed to work the big cage alone. She had been sixteen, and it had been another full year before she had been permitted to work an audience.

For Jo, there had never been any home but the circus. She had been born during the winter break, had been tucked into her parents' trailer the following spring to spend her first year and each subsequent one of her life thereafter on the road. She had inherited both her fascination and her flair with animals from her father, her style and grace of movement from her mother. Though she had lost both parents fifteen years before, they continued to influence her. Their legacy to her had been a world of restlessness, a world of fantasies. She had grown up playing with lion cubs, riding elephants, wearing spangles and traveling like a gypsy.

Jo glanced down at a cluster of daffodils growing by the side of Prescott's winter office and smiled. She remembered planting them when she had been thirteen and in love with a tumbler. She remembered, too, the man who had stooped beside her, offering advice on bulb planting and broken hearts. As Jo thought of Frank Prescott, her smile grew sad.

"I still can't believe he's gone," she murmured as she and Duffy moved inside.

Duffy's office was sparsely furnished with a wooden desk, metal filing cabinets and two spindly chairs. A collage of posters adorned the walls. They promised the amazing, the astounding, the incredible: elephants that danced, men who flew through the air, beautiful girls who spun by their teeth, raging tigers that rode horseback. Tumblers, clowns, lions, strong men, fat ladies, boys who could balance on their forefingers; they brought the magic of the circus into the drab little room.

As Jo glanced over at a narrow pine door, Duffy followed her gaze. "I keep expecting him to come busting through there with some crazy new idea," he mumbled as he began to fiddle with his prize possession, an automatic coffee maker.

"Do you?" With a sigh Jo straddled a chair, then rested her chin on its back. "We all miss him. It's not going to seem the same without him this year." She looked up suddenly, and her eyes were angry. "He wasn't an old man, Duffy. Heart attacks should be for old men." She brooded into space, touched again with the injustice of Frank Prescott's death.

He had been barely into his fifties and full of laughter and simple kindness. Jo had loved him and trusted him without reservation. At his death she had grieved for him more acutely than she had for her own parents. In her longest memory he had been the core of her life.

"It's been nearly six months," Duffy said gruffly as he studied her face. When Jo glanced up, he stuck out a mug of coffee.

"I know." She took the mug, letting it warm her hands in the chilly March morning. Resolutely, she shook off the mood. Frank would not have wanted to leave sadness behind. Jo studied the coffee, then sipped. It was predictably dreadful. "Rumor has it we're following last year's route to the letter. Thirteen states." Jo smiled, watching Duffy wince over his coffee before he downed it. "Not superstitious, are you?" She grinned, knowing he kept a four-leaf clover in his billfold.

"*Pah!*" he said indignantly, coloring under his freckles. He set down his empty cup, then moved around his desk and sat behind it. When he folded his hands on the yellow blotter, Jo knew he was getting down to business. Through the open window she could hear the band rehearsing. "We should be in Ocala by six tomorrow," he began. Dutifully, Jo nodded. "Should have the tents up before nine."

"The parade should be over by ten, and the matinee will start at two," Jo finished with a smile. "Duffy, you're not going to ask me to work the menagerie in the side show again, are you?"

"Should be a good crowd," he replied, adroitly skirting her question. "Bonzo predicts clear skies."

"Bonzo should stick with pratfalls and unicycles." She watched as Duffy chewed on the stub of a now dead cigar. "Okay," she said firmly, "let's have it."

"Someone's going to be joining us in Ocala, at least temporarily." He pursed his lips as his eyes met Jo's. His were blue, faded with age. "I don't know if he'll finish out the season with us."

"Oh, Duffy, not some first of mayer we have to break in this late?" Jo demanded, using the circus term for novice. "What is he, some energetic writer who wants an epic on the vanishing tent circus? He'll spend a few weeks as a roustabout and swear he knows all there is to know about it."

"I don't think he'll be working as a roustabout," Duffy muttered. Striking a match, he coaxed the cigar back to life. Jo frowned, watching the smoke struggle toward the ceiling.

"It's a bit late to work in a new act now, isn't it?"

"He's not a performer." Duffy swore lightly under his breath, then met Jo's eyes again. "He owns us."

For a moment Jo said nothing. She sat unmoving, as Duffy had seen her from time to time when she trained a young cat. "No!" She rose suddenly, shaking her head. "Not him. Not now. Why does he have to come? What does he want here?"

"It's his circus," Duffy reminded her. His voice was both rough and sympathetic.

"It'll never be his circus," Jo retorted passionately. Her eyes lit and glowed with a temper she rarely let have sway. "It's Frank's circus."

"Frank's dead," Duffy stated in a quiet, final tone. "Now the circus belongs to his son."

"Son?" Jo countered. She lifted her fingers to press them against her temple. Slowly, she moved to the window. Outside, the sun was pouring over the heads of troupers. She watched the members of the trapeze act, in thick robes worn over their tights, head toward the ring barn. The chatter of mixed languages was so familiar she failed to notice it. She placed her palms on the window sill and with a little sigh, steadied her temper. "What sort of son is it who never bothers to visit his father? In thirty years he never came to see Frank. He never wrote. He didn't even come to the funeral." Jo swallowed the tears of anger that rose to her throat and thickened her voice. "Why should he come now?"

"You've got to learn that life's a two-sided coin, kiddo," Duffy said briskly. "You weren't even alive thirty years ago. You don't know why Frank's wife up and left him or why the boy never visited."

"He's not a boy, Duffy, he's a man." Jo turned back, and he saw that she again had herself under control. "He's thirty-one, thirty-two years old now, a very successful attorney with a fancy Chicago office. He's very wealthy, did you know?" A small smile played on her lips but failed to reach her eyes. "And not just from court cases and legal fees; there's quite a lot of money on his mother's side. Nice, quiet, old money. I can't understand what a rich city lawyer would want with a tent circus."

Duffy shrugged his broad, round shoulders. "Could be he wants a tax shelter. Could be he wants to ride an elephant. Could be anything. He might want to take inventory and sell us off, piece by piece."

"Oh, Duffy, no!" Emotion flew back into Jo's face. "He couldn't do that."

"The heck he couldn't," Duffy muttered as he stubbed out his cigar. "He can do as he pleases. If he wants to liquidate, he liquidates."

"But we have contracts through October...."

"You're too smart for that, Jo." Duffy frowned, scratching his rim of hair. "He can buy them off or let them play through. He's a lawyer. He can figure the way out of a contract if he wants to. He can wait till August when we start to negotiate again and let them all lapse.'' Seeing Jo's distress, he backpedaled. ''Listen, kiddo, I didn't say he was going to sell, I said he *could.*''

Jo ran a hand through her hair. ''There must be something we can do.''

''We can show a profit by the end of the season,'' Duffy said wryly. ''We can show the new owner what we have to offer. I think it's important that he sees we're not just a mud show but a profitable three-ring circus with class acts. He should see what Frank built, how he lived, what he wanted to do. I think,'' Duffy added, watching Jo's face, ''that you should be in charge of his education.''

''Me?'' Jo was too incredulous to be angry. ''Why? You're better qualified in the public relations department than I am. I train lions, not lawyers.'' She could not keep the hint of scorn from her voice.

''You were closer to Frank than anyone. And there isn't anyone here who knows this circus better than you.'' Again he frowned. ''And you've got brains. Never thought much use would come of all those fancy books you read, but maybe I was wrong.''

''Duffy.'' Her lips curved into a smile. ''Just because I like to read Shakespeare doesn't mean I can deal with Keane Prescott. Even thinking about him makes me furious. How will I act when I meet him face to face?''

"Well." Duffy shrugged before he pursed his lips. "If you don't think you can handle it . . ."

"I didn't say I *couldn't* handle it," Jo muttered.

"Of course, if you're afraid . . ."

"I'm not afraid of anything, and I'm certainly not afraid of some Chicago lawyer who doesn't know sawdust from tanbark." Sticking her hands in her pockets, she paced the length of the small room. "If Keane Prescott, attorney-at-law, wants to spend his summer with the circus, I'll do my best to make it a memorable one."

"Nicely," Duffy cautioned as Jo moved to the door.

"Duffy," she paused and gave him an innocent smile. "You know what a gentle touch I have." To prove it, Jo slammed the door behind her.

Dawn was hovering over the horizon as the circus caravan drew up in a large, grassy field. Colors were just a promise in a pale gray sky. In the distance was grove upon grove of orange trees. As Jo stepped from the cab of her truck, the fragrance met her. It's a perfect day, she decided, then took a long, greedy breath. To her, there was no more beautiful sight than dawn struggling to life.

The air was vaguely chilly. She zipped up her gray sweat jacket as she watched the rest of the circus troupe pouring out of their trucks and cars

and trailers. The morning quiet was soon shattered by voices. Work began immediately. As the
Big Top canvas was being unrolled out of the
spool truck, Jo went to see how her lions had
fared the fifty-mile journey.

Three handlers unloaded the traveling cages.
Buck had been with Jo the longest. He had
worked for her father, and during the interim
between his death and Jo's professional debut, he
had worked up a small act with four male lions.
His shyness had made his retirement from performing a relief. To Buck, two people were a
crowd. He stood six-feet-four, and his build was
powerful enough for him to pad the sideshow
from time to time as Hercules the Strong Man.
He had an impressive head of wild blond hair and
a full, curling beard. His hands were wide, with
thick, strong fingers, but Jo remembered their
gentleness when the two of them had delivered a
lioness of a pair of cubs.

Pete's small frame seemed puny beside Buck's.
He was of indeterminable age. Jo guessed between forty and fifty, but she was never certain.
He was a quiet man with skin like polished ma-
hogany and a rich, low-pitched voice. He had
come to Jo five years before, asking for a job.
She had never asked where he had come from,
and he had never told her. He wore a fielder's cap
and was never seen without a wad of gum moving gently in his teeth. He read Jo's books and
was the undisputed king of the poker table.

Gerry was nineteen and eager. He was nearly six feet and still carried the lankiness of his youth. His mother sewed, and his father was a souvenir salesman, or a candy butcher, as circus jargon had it. Working the big cage was Gerry's dream, and because it had been hers, Jo had finally agreed to tutor him.

"How are my babies?" she demanded as she approached. At each cage she paused and soothed a nervous cat, calling each by name until they had settled. "They've traveled well. Hamlet's still edgy, but it's his first year on the road."

"He's a mean one," Buck muttered, watching Jo move from cage to cage.

"Yes, I know," she replied absently. "He's smart, too." She had twisted her hair into one thick braid and now tossed it to her back. "Look, here come some towners." A few cars and a smattering of bikes drew into the field.

These were the people from the outlying towns who wanted to see a Big Top raised, who wanted to see the circus, if only for a moment, from the other side. Some would watch while others would lend a hand with tent poles, stretching canvas and rigging. They would earn a show pass and an unforgettable experience.

"Keep them clear of the cages," Jo ordered, nodding to Pete before she moved toward the still flaccid canvas. Buck lumbered beside her.

The field was alive with ropes and wire and people. Six elephants were harnessed but idle, with their handlers standing by the stake line. As workers pulled on guy ropes, the dusky brown canvas billowed up like a giant mushroom.

The poles were positioned—side, quarter, center—while the canvas muffled the sounds of scrambling workers. In the east the sun was rising fast, streaking the sky with pink. There were shouted instructions from the head canvas man, laughter from adventuresome boys and an occasional oath. As the quarter poles were driven into the sag of canvas, Jo signaled Maggie, the large African elephant. Obligingly, Maggie lowered her trunk. Jo stepped nimbly into the *u*, then scrambled onto the wide, gray back.

The sun grew higher by the second, shooting the first streams of light onto the field. The scent of orange blossoms mingled with the odor of leather harnesses. Jo had watched the canvas rise under a lightening sky countless times. Each time it was special, and the first raising each season was the most special of all. Maggie lifted her head and trumpeted as if pleased to be around for another season. With a laugh Jo reached back and swatted her rough, wrinkled rump. She felt free and fresh and incredibly alive. If there were a moment, she thought suddenly, that I could capture and bottle, it would be this one. Then, when I'm very old, I could take it out and feel young again. Smiling, she glanced down at the people swarming below her.

Her attention was caught by a man who stood by a coil of cable. Typically, she noted his build first. A well-proportioned body was essential to a performer. He was lean and stood straight. She noted he had good shoulders but doubted if there was much muscle in his arms. Though he was dressed casually in jeans, *city* stood out all over him. His hair was a dark, rich blond, and the early breeze had disturbed it so that it teased his forehead. He was clean-shaven, with a narrow, firm-jawed face. It was an attractive face. It was not, Jo mused, smoothly handsome like Vito the wire walker's but more aware, more demanding. Jo liked the face, liked the shape of the long, un-smiling mouth, liked the hint of bone beneath his tawny skin. Most of all she liked the directness of the amber eyes that stared back at her. They're like Ari's, she observed, thinking of her favorite lion. She was certain that he had been watching her long before she had looked down. Knowing this, Jo was impressed with his unselfconscious-ness. He continued to stare, making no effort to camouflage his interest. She laughed, unper-turbed, and tossed her braid from her shoulder.

"Want a ride?" she called out. Too many strangers had walked in and out of her world for her to be aloof. She watched his brow lift in ac-knowledgment of her offer. She would see if it was only his eyes that were like Ari's. "Maggie won't hurt you. She's gentle as a lamb, just bigger.'' Instantly, she saw he had understood the challenge. He walked across the grass until he stood beside her. He moved well, she noted. Jo tapped Maggie's side with the bull hook she carried. Wearily, the elephant knelt down on her trunklike front legs. Jo held out her hand. With an agility that surprised her, the man mounted the elephant and slid into place behind her.

For a moment she said nothing, a bit stunned by the trembling that had coursed up her arm as her palm had met his. The contact had been brief. Jo decided she had imagined it. "Up, Maggie," she said, giving her mount another tap. With an elephantine sigh, Maggie obeyed, rocking her passengers gently from side to side.

"Do you always pick up strange men?" the voice behind her inquired. It was a smooth, well-keyed voice, a good pitchman's voice.

Jo grinned over her shoulder. "Maggie's doing the picking up."

"So she is. Are you aware that she's remarkably uncomfortable?"

Jo laughed with genuine enjoyment. "You should try riding her a few miles in a street parade while keeping a smile on your face."

"I'll pass. Are you in charge of her?"

"Maggie? No, but I know how to handle her. You have eyes like one of my cats," she told him. "I like them. And since you seemed to be interested in Maggie and me, I asked you up."

This time it was he who laughed. Jo twisted her head, wanting to see his face. There was humor in his eyes now, and his teeth were white and straight. Liking his smile, she answered with one of her own. "Fascinating. You asked me to take a ride on an elephant because I have eyes like your cat's. And no offense to the lady beneath me, but I was looking at you."

"Oh?" Jo pursed her lips in thought. "Why?"

For several seconds he studied her in silence. "Strange, I believe you really don't know."

"I wouldn't ask if I did," she returned, shifting her weight slightly. "It would be a waste of time to ask a question if I knew the answer." She shifted again and turned away from him. "Hold on now. Maggie's got to earn her bale of hay."

The poles hung between the canvas and the ground at forty-five degree angles. Quickly the elephant's chains were hooked to the metal rings at the base of the quarter poles. Jo urged Maggie forward in unison with her coworkers. Poles skidded along the ground, then up into place, pushing the canvas with it. The Big Top billowed to life under the early morning sky.

Her job done, Maggie moved through the flaps and into the light. "Beautiful, isn't it?" Jo murmured. "It's born fresh every day."

Vito walked by, calling out to Jo in Italian. Sending him a wave, she called back in his own language, then signaled to Maggie to kneel again. Jo waited until her passenger had dismounted

before she slid off. It surprised her, when they
stood face to face, that he was so tall. Tilting
back her head, she judged him to be only two
inches shy of Buck.

"You looked shorter when I was up on Maggie," she told him with her usual candor.

"You looked taller."

Jo chuckled, patting Maggie behind the ear.
"Will you see the show?" She knew that she
wanted him to, knew as well that she wanted to
see him again. She found this both strange and
intriguing. Men had always taken a second place
to her cats, and towners had never interested her.

"Yes, I'm going to see the show." There was a
slight smile on his face, but he was studying her
thoughtfully. "Do you perform?"

"I have an act with my cats."

"I see. Somehow I pictured you in an aerial
act, flying from the trapeze."

She sent him an easy smile. "My mother was
an aerialist." Someone called her name, and
looking, Jo saw Maggie was needed for raising
the sideshow tent. "I have to go. I hope you like
the show."

He took her hand before she could lead Maggie away. Jo stood still, again surprised by a
trembling up her arm. "I'd like to see you tonight."

Glancing up, she met his eyes. They were direct and unselfconscious. "Why?" The question

was sincere. Jo knew she wanted to see him as well but was unsure why.

This time he did not laugh. Gently, he ran a finger down the length of her braid. "Because you're beautiful, and you intrigue me."

"Oh." Jo considered. She had never thought of herself as beautiful. Striking, perhaps, in her costume, surrounded by her cats, but in jeans, without makeup, she doubted it. Still, it was an interesting thought. "All right, if there's no trouble with the cats. Ari hasn't been well."

A smile played at the corners of his mouth. "I'm sorry to hear that."

There was another loud summons for Jo, and both looked toward it. "I see you're needed," he said with a nod. "Perhaps you could point out Bill Duffy for me before you go."

"Duffy?" Jo repeated, surprised. "You can't be looking for a job?" There was incredulity in her voice, and he grinned.

"Why can't I?"

"Because you don't fit any of the types."

"Are there types?" he asked, both interested and amused. Jo shook her head in annoyance.

"Yes, of course, and you don't fit into any of them."

"Actually, I'm not looking for a job, so to speak," he told her, still smiling. "But I am looking for Bill Duffy."

It was against Jo's nature to probe. Privacy was both guarded and respected in the circus.

Shielding her eyes with her hand, Jo looked
around until she spotted Duffy supervising the
raising of the cookhouse tent. "There," she said,
pointing. "Duffy's the one with the red checked
jacket. He still dresses like an outside talker."

"A what?"

"You'd call it a barker, I imagine." With easy
grace she mounted the patient Maggie. "That's
a towner's term, not a circus one." She smiled at
him, then urged Maggie into a walk. "Tell Duffy
Jo said to give you a pass," she called over her
shoulder, then waved and turned away.

Dawn was over, and it was morning.

Chapter Two

Jo stood at the back door of the Big Top waiting for her cue. Beside her was Jamie Carter, alias Topo. He was a third generation clown and wore his bright face and orange wig naturally. He was young and limber and used these traits as well as his makeup to bring enthusiasm to his craft. To Jo, Jamie was more brother than friend. He was tall and thin, and under his greasepaint his face was mobile and pleasant. He and Jo had grown up together.

"Did she say anything?" Jamie demanded for the third time. With a sigh, Jo tossed closed the flap of the tent. Inside, clowns were performing around the hippodrome track while hands set up the big cage.

"Carmen said nothing. I don't know why you waste your time." Her voice was sharp, and Jamie bristled.

"I don't expect you to understand," he said with great dignity. His thin shoulders drew straight under his red polka dot shirt. "After all, Ari's the closest you've come to being involved with the opposite sex."

"That's very cute," Jo replied, unoffended by the jibe. Her annoyance stemmed from seeing Jamie make a fool of himself over Carmen Gribalti, the middle sister of the flying Gribaltis. She was darkly beautiful, graceful, talented, selfish and sublimely indifferent to Jamie. Looking into his happy, painted face and moody eyes, Jo's irritation dissipated. "She probably hasn't had a chance to answer the note you sent her," she soothed. "The first day of a new season's always wild."

"I suppose," Jamie muttered with a grudging shrug. "I don't know what she sees in Vito."

Jo thought of the wire walker's dark, cocky looks and rippling muscles. Wisely, she refrained from mentioning them. "Who can account for taste?" She gave him a smacking kiss on his round, red nose. "Personally, I get all wobbly when I see a man with thick, orange hair."

Jamie grinned. "Proves you know what to look for in a man."

Turning, Jo lifted the flap again, noting Jamie's cue was nearly upon them. "Did you happen to notice a towner hanging around today?"

"Only a couple dozen of them," Jamie answered dryly as he lifted the pail of confetti he used to finish the gag now being performed inside.

Jo shot him a half-hearted glare. "Not the usual type. About thirty, I think," she continued. "Wearing jeans and a T-shirt. He was tall, six-one, six-two," she went on as laughter poured out of the open flap to drown out her words. "He had dark blond straight hair."

"Yeah, I saw him." Jamie nudged her out of his way and prepared to make his entrance. "He was going into the red wagon with Duffy." With a wild, high-pitched scream, Topo the clown bounded into the Big Top in size fifteen tennis shoes, brandishing his bucket of confetti.

Thoughtfully, Jo watched Jamie chase three other clowns around the track. It was odd, she thought, for Duffy to take a towner into the administration trailer. He had said he wasn't looking for a job. He wasn't a drifter; there was an unmistakable air of stability about him. He wasn't a circus hand from another show, either. His palm had been too smooth. And, her mind added as she vaulted onto Babette, a pure white mare, there had been an undeniable aura of urbanity about him. Success, as well, she thought. And authority. No, he had not been looking for a job.

Jo shrugged, annoyed that a stranger was crowding into her thoughts. It irritated her further that she had scanned the crowds for him during the parade and that even now she wondered if he sat somewhere in the circular arena. He hadn't been at the matinee. Jo patted the mare's neck absently, then straightened as she heard the ringmaster's whistle.

"Ladies and gentlemen," he called in deep, musical tones. "Presenting the most spectacular exhibition of animal subjugation under the Big Top. Jovilette, Queen of the Jungle Cats!"

Jo nudged Babette with her heels and raced into the arena. The applause rose to meet her as the audience appreciated the dashing figure she cut. Swathed in a black cape, raven hair flying free under a glittering tiara, she galloped bareback on the snow white mare. In each hand she held a long, thin whip, which she cracked alternately overhead. At the entrance to the big cage she leaped from the still racing horse. While Babette galloped out of the back door and into the care of a handler, Jo shifted both whips into one hand, then removed the cape with a flourish. Her costume was a close-fitting, one-piece jumpsuit, dazzling in white and spangled with gold sequins. In dramatic contrast, her hair hung straight and severe down her back.

Make an entrance, Frank had always said. And Jovilette made an entrance.

The twelve cats were already in the cage, banding its inside edge as they perched on blue and white pedestals. Entering the main cage appeared routine to the audience, but Jo knew it was one of the most dangerous moments of the act. To enter, she had to pass directly between two cats as she moved from the safety cage to the

main arena. She always stationed her best behaved cats there, but if one was irritated, or even
playful, he could easily strike out with a powerful paw. Even with sharp claws retracted, the
damage could be deadly.

She entered swiftly and was surrounded by cats
on all sides. Her spangles and tiara caught the
lights and played with them as she began to move
around the cage, cracking the whip for show-
manship while using her voice to command the
cats to rise on their haunches. She moved them
through their routine, adjusting the timing to
compensate for any feline reluctance, letting one
trick begin where the last ended.

Jo disliked overdone propping, preferring action and movement. The contrast of the big,
tawny cats and the small white and gold woman
were the best props available to her. She used
them well. Hers was a *picture act,* relying on style
and flash, rather than a *fighting act,* which em-
phasized the ferocity of the big cats by employ-
ing blank-bulleted guns and rehearsed charges, or
bounces. Her confidence transmitted itself to the
audience, making her handling of the cats appear effortless. In truth, her body was coiled for
any danger, and her mind was focused so in-
tently on her cats, there might have been no audience at all.

She stood between two high pedestals as the
cats leaped over her head from both directions.
They set up a light breeze, which stirred her hair.

They roared when she cued them, setting up an
echoing din. Now and then one reached out to
paw at the stock of her whip, and she stopped
him with a quick command. She sent her best
leaper through a hoop of flame and coaxed her
best balancer to walk on a glistening silver ball.
She ended to waves of applause by trotting Merlin around the hippodrome track.

At the back door Merlin jumped into a wheel
cage and was turned over to Pete. "Nice show,"
he said as he handed her a long chenille robe.
"Smooth as silk."

"Thanks." Cold, she bundled into the robe.
The spring night was frigid in contrast to the hot
lights and heat in the big cage. "Listen, Pete, tell
Gerry he can feed the cats tonight. They're be-
having themselves."

Pete snapped his gum and chuckled. "Won't
he be riding high tonight." As he moved to the
truck that would pull the cage to the cat area, Jo
called after him.

"Pete." She bit her lip, then shrugged when he
twisted his head. "You'll keep an eye on him,
won't you?"

Pete grinned and climbed into the cab of the
truck. "Who you worried about, Jo? Those big
cats or that skinny boy?"

"Both," she answered. The rhinestones in her
tiara sparkled as she tossed her head and laughed.
Knowing she had nearly an hour before the finale parade, Jo walked away from the Big Top.

She thought of wandering to the cookhouse for some coffee. Mentally, she began replaying every segment of her act. It had gone well, she thought, pleased with the timing and the flow. If Pete had said it had been smooth, Jo knew it had. She had heard his criticisms more than once over the past five years. True, Hamlet had tested her once or twice, but no one knew that but Jo and the cat. She doubted if anyone but Buck would have seen that he had given her trouble. Closing her eyes a moment, Jo rolled her shoulders, loosening tight, tensed muscles.

"That's quite an act you have."

Jo whirled around at the sound of the voice. She could feel her heart rate accelerate. Though she wondered at her interest in a man she barely knew, Jo was aware that she had been waiting for him. There was a quick surge of pleasure as she watched him approach, and she allowed it to show on her face.

"Hello." She saw that he smoked a cigar, but unlike Duffy's, his was long and slim. Again she admired the elegance of his hands. "Did you like the show?"

He stopped in front of her, then studied her face with a thoroughness that made her wonder if her makeup had smeared. Then he gave a small, surprised laugh and shook his head. "Do you know," he began, "when you told me this morning that you did an act with cats, I had Siamese in mind rather than African."

"Siamese?" Jo repeated blankly, then laughed. "House cats?" He brushed her hair behind her back while Jo giggled at the thought of coaxing a Siamese to jump through a flaming hoop.

"From my point of view," he told her as he let a strand of her hair linger between his fingers, "it made more sense than a little thing like you walking into a cage with a dozen lions."

"I'm not little," Jo corrected good-naturedly. "Besides, size hardly matters to twelve lions."

"No, I suppose it doesn't." He lifted his eyes from her hair and met hers. Jo continued to smile, enjoying looking at him. "Why do you do it?" he asked suddenly.

Jo gave him a curious look. "Why? Because it's my job."

By the way he studied her, Jo could see that he was not satisfied with the simplicity of her answer. "Perhaps I should ask *how* you became a lion tamer."

"Trainer," Jo corrected automatically. To her left, she could hear the audience's muffled applause. "The Beirots are starting," she said with a glance toward the sound. "You shouldn't miss their act. They're first-rate acrobats."

"Don't you want to tell me?" His voice was soft.

She lifted a brow, seeing that he truly wanted to know. "Why, it's not a secret. My father was a trainer, and I have a knack for working with cats. It just followed." Jo had never thought about her career past this point, and she shrugged it aside. "You shouldn't waste your ticket standing out here. You can stand by the back door and watch the rest of the act." Jo turned to lead the way to the performer's entrance but stopped when his hand took hers.

He stepped forward until their bodies were nearly touching. Jo could feel the heat from his as she watched his face. Her heart was thudding in a quick, steady rhythm. She could hear it vibrate through her the same way it did when she approached a new cat for the first time. Here was something new, something untested. She tingled with the excitement of the unknown when he lifted his hand to touch her cheek. She did not move but let the warmth spread while she watched him carefully, gauging him. Her eyes were wide, curious and unafraid.

"Are you going to kiss me?" she asked in a tone that expressed more interest than desire.

His eyes lit with humor and glittered in the dim light. "I had given it some thought," he answered. "Do you have any objections?"

Jo considered a moment, dropping her eyes to his mouth. She liked its shape and wondered how it would feel against hers. He brought her no closer. One hand still held hers while the other slid around to cradle her neck. Jo shifted her gaze until their eyes met again. "No," she decided. "I haven't any objections."

The corners of his mouth twitched as he tightened his hold slightly on the base of her neck. Slowly, he lowered his head toward hers. Curious and a bit wary, Jo kept her eyes open, watching his. She knew from experience that you could tell more about people and about cats from the eyes. To her surprise, his remained open as well, even as their lips met.

It was a gentle kiss, without pressure, only a whisper of a touch. Amazed, Jo thought she felt the ground tremble under her feet. Dimly, she wondered if the elephants were being led by. But it can't be time, she thought in confusion. His lips moved lightly over hers, and his eyes remained steady. Jo's pulse drummed under her skin. They stood, barely touching, as the Big Top throbbed with noise behind them. Lazily, he traced her lips with the tip of his tongue, teasing them open. Still there was no demand in the kiss, only testing. Unhurried, confident, he explored her mouth while Jo felt her breath accelerating. A soft moan escaped her as her lids fluttered down.

For an instant she surrendered utterly to him, to the new sensations swimming through her. She leaned against him, straining toward pleasure, sighing with it as the kiss lingered.

He drew her away, but their faces remained close. Dizzily, Jo realized that she had risen to her toes to compensate for their difference in height.

His hand was still light on the back of her neck. His eyes were gold in the darkening night.

"What an incredible female you are, Jovilette," he murmured. "One surprise after another."

Jo felt stunningly alive. Her skin seemed to tingle with new feelings. She smiled. "I don't know your name."

He laughed, releasing her neck to take her other hand in his. Before he could speak, Duffy called out from the direction of the Big Top. Jo turned to watch as he moved toward them in his quick, rolling walk.

"Well, well, well," he said in his jolly, rough voice. "I didn't know you two had met. Has Jo been showing you around already?" Reaching them, he squeezed Jo's shoulder. "Knew I could count on you, kiddo." Jo glanced at him in puzzlement, but he continued before she could form a question. "Yes, sir, this little girl puts on quite a show, doesn't she? Always a grabber. And she knows this circus like the back of her hand. Born and raised to it," he continued. Jo relaxed. She recognized that Duffy was into one of his spiels, and there was no stopping him. "Yessiree, any questions you got, you just ask our Jo, and she'll tell you. 'Course, I'm always at your disposal, too. Anything I can tell you about the books or accounts or contracts and the like, you just let me know." Duffy puffed twice on his cigar as Jo felt her first hint of unease.

Why was Duffy rambling about books and contracts? Jo glanced at the man who still held her hands in his. He was watching Duffy with an easy, amused smile.

"Are you a bookkeeper?" Jo asked, perplexed. Duffy laughed and patted her head.

"You know Mr. Prescott's a lawyer, Jo. Don't miss your cue." He gave them both a friendly nod and toddled off.

Jo had stiffened almost imperceptibly at Duffy's offhand information, but Keane had felt it. His brows lowered as he studied her. "Now you know my name."

"Yes." All warmth fled from Jo. Her voice was as cool as her blood. "Would you let go of my hands, Mr. Prescott?"

After a brief hesitation Keane inclined his head and obliged. Jo stuffed her hands quickly into the pockets of her robe. "Don't you think we've progressed to the first name stage of our relationship, Jo?"

"I assure you, Mr. Prescott, if I had known who you were, we wouldn't have progressed at all." Jo's words were stiff with dignity. Inside, though she tried to ignore it, she felt betrayal, anger, humiliation. All pleasure had died from the evening. Now the kiss that had left her feeling clean and alive seemed cheap and shabby. No, she would not use his first name, she vowed. She would never use it. "If you'll excuse me, I have some things to do before my cue."

"Why the turnaround?" he asked, halting her with a hand on her arm. "Don't you like lawyers?"

Coldly, Jo studied him. She wondered how it was possible that she had completely misjudged the man she had met that morning. "I don't categorize people, Mr. Prescott."

"I see." Keane's tone became detached, his eyes assessing. "Then it would appear that you have an aversion to my name. Should I assume you hold a grudge against my father?"

Jo's eyes glittered with quick fury. She jerked her arm from his hold. "Frank Prescott was the most generous, the kindest, most unselfish man I've ever known. I don't even associate you with Frank, Mr. Prescott. You have no right to him." Though it was nearly impossible, Jo forced herself to speak in a normal tone of voice. She would not shout and draw anyone's attention. This would be kept strictly between Keane Prescott and herself. "It would have been much better if you had told me who you were right away, then there would have been no mix-up."

"Is that what we've had?" he countered mildly. "A mix-up?"

His cool tone was nearly Jo's undoing. He watched her with a dispassionate curiosity that tempted her to slap him. She fought to keep her fury from spilling over into her voice. "You have no right to Frank's circus, Mr. Prescott," she managed quietly. "Leaving it to you is the only thing I've ever faulted him for." Knowing her control was slipping, Jo whirled, running across the grass until she merged with the darkness.

Chapter Three

The morning was surprisingly warm. There were no trees to block the sun, and the smell of the earth was strong. The circus had moved north in the early hours. All the usual scents merged into the aroma of circus: canvas, leather, sweating horses, greasepaint and powder, coffee and oil-cloth. The trailers and trucks sat in the accustomed spots, forming the "back yard" that would always take the same formation each time the circus made a stop along the thousands of miles it traveled. The flag over the cookhouse tent signaled that lunch was being served. The Big Top stood waiting for the matinee.

Rose hurried along the midway toward the animal cages. Her dark hair was pinned neatly in a bun at the back of her neck. Her big brown eyes darted about searchingly, while her mouth sat softly in a pout. She was wrapped in a terry cloth robe and wore tennis shoes over her tights. When she saw Jo standing in front of Ari's cage, she waved and broke into a half-run. Watching her, Jo shifted her attention from Ari. Rose was always a diversion, and Jo felt in need of one.

"Jo!" She waved again as if Jo had not seen her the first time, then came to a breathless halt. "Jo, I only have a few minutes. Hello, Ari," she added out of politeness. "I was looking for Jamie."

"Yes, I gathered." Jo smiled, knowing Rose had set her heart on capturing Topo's alter ego. And if he had any sense, she thought, he'd let himself be caught instead of pining over Carmen. Silly, she decided, dismissing all affairs of the heart. Lions were easier to understand. "I haven't seen him all morning, Rose. Maybe he's rehearsing."

"Drooling over Carmen, more likely," Rose muttered, sending a sulky glare in the direction of the Gribalti trailer. "He makes a fool of himself."

"That's what he's paid for," Jo reminded her, but Rose did not respond to the humor. Jo sighed. She had a true affection for Rose. She was bright and fun and without pretentions. "Rose," she said, keeping her voice both light and kind. "Don't give up on him. He's a little slow, you know," she explained. "He's just a bit dazzled by Carmen right now. It'll pass."

"I don't know why I bother," she grumbled, but Jo saw the dark mood was already passing. Rose was a creature of quick passions that flared and soon died. "He's not so very handsome, you know."

"No," Jo agreed. "But he has a cute nose."

"Lucky for him I like red," Rose returned and grinned. "Ah, now we're speaking of handsome," she murmured as her eyes drifted from Jo. "Who is this?"

At the question, Jo glanced over her shoulder. The humor fled from her eyes. "That's the owner," she said colorlessly.

"Keane Prescott? No one told me he was so handsome. Or so tall," she added, admiring him openly as he crossed the back yard. Jo noted that Rose always became more Mexican around men. "Such shoulders. Lucky for Jamie I'm a one-man woman."

"Lucky for you your mama can't hear you," Jo muttered, earning an elbow in the ribs.

"But he comes here, *amiga,* and he looks at you. La, la, my papa would have Jamie to the altar *pronto* if he looked at me that way."

"You're an idiot," Jo snapped, annoyed.

"Ah, Jo," Rose said with mock despair. "I am a romantic."

Jo was helpless against the smile that tugged at her lips. Her eyes were laughing when she glanced up and met Keane's. Hastily, she struggled to dampen their brilliance, turning her mouth into a sober line.

"Good morning, Jovilette." He spoke her name too easily, she thought, as if he had been saying it for years.

"Good morning, Mr. Prescott," she returned. Rose gave a loud, none-too-subtle cough. "This is Rose Sanches."

"It's a pleasure, Mr. Prescott." Rose extended a hand, trying out a smile she had been saving for Jamie. "I heard you were traveling with us."

Keane accepted the hand and smiled in return. Jo noticed with annoyance that it was the same easy, disarming smile of the stranger she had met the morning before. "Hello, Rose, it's nice to meet you."

Seeing her friend's Mexican blood heat her cheeks, Jo intervened. She would not permit Keane Prescott to make a conquest here. "Rose, you only have ten minutes to get back and into makeup."

"Holy cow!" she said, forgetting her attempt at sophistication. "I've got to run." She began to do so, then called over her shoulder, "Don't tell Jamie I was looking for him, the pig!" She ran a little further, then turned and ran backwards. "I'll look for him later," she said with a laugh, then turned back and streaked toward the midway.

Keane watched her dart across the compound while holding up the long skirts of her robe in one hand. "Charming."

"She's only eighteen," Jo offered before she could stop herself.

When Keane turned to her, his look was one of amusement. "I see," he said. "I'll take that information under advisement. And what does the eighteen-year-old Rose do?'' he asked, slipping his thumbs into the front pockets of his jeans. ''Wrestle alligators?''

''No.'' Jo returned without batting an eye. ''Rose is Serpentina, your premier sideshow attraction. The snake charmer.'' She was pleased with the incredulous look that passed over his face. It was replaced quickly, however, with one of genuine humor.

''Perfect.'' He brushed Jo's hair from her cheek before she could protest by word or action. ''Cobras?'' he asked, ignoring the flash in her eyes.

''And boa constrictors,'' she returned sweetly. Jo brushed the dust from the knees of her faded jeans. ''Now, if you'll excuse me . . .''

''No, I don't think so.'' Keane's voice was cool, but she recognized the underlying authority. She did her best not to struggle against it. He *was* the owner, she reminded herself.

''Mr. Prescott,'' she began, banking down hard on the urge to mutiny. ''I'm very busy. I have to get ready for the afternoon show.''

''You've got an hour and a half until you're on,'' he countered smoothly. ''I think you might spare me a portion of that time. You've been assigned to show me around. Why don't we start now?'' The tone of the question left room for only one answer. Jo's mind fidgeted in search of a way out.

Tilting her head back, she met his eyes. He won't be easy to beat, she concluded, studying his steady, measuring gaze. I'd better study his moves more carefully before I start a battle. "Where would you like to begin?" she asked aloud.

"With you."

Keane's easy answer brought a deep frown to Jo's brows. "I don't understand what you mean."

For a moment Keane watched her. There was no coyness or guile in her eyes as they looked into his. "No, I can see you don't," he agreed with a nod. "Let's start with your cats."

"Oh." Jo's frown cleared instantly. "All right." She watched as he pulled out a thin cigar, waiting until the flame of his lighter licked the tip before speaking. "I have thirteen—seven males, six females. They're all African lions between four-and-a-half and twenty-two years."

"I thought you worked with twelve," Keane commented as he dropped his lighter into his pocket.

"That's right, but Ari's retired." Turning, Jo indicated the large male lion dozing in a cage. "He travels with me because he always has, but I don't work him anymore. He's twenty-two, the oldest. My father kept him, even though he was born in captivity, because he was born the same day I was." Jo sighed, and her voice became softer. "He's the last of my father's stock. I couldn't sell him to a zoo. It seemed like shoving an old relative into a home and abandoning him. He's been with this circus every day of his life, just as I have. His name is Hebrew for *lion*." Jo laughed, forgetting the man beside her as she sifted through memories. "My father always gave his cats names that meant lion somehow or other. Leo, Leonard, Leonara. Ari was a first-class leaper in his prime. He could climb, too; some cats won't. I could teach Ari anything. Smart cat, aren't you, Ari?" The altered tone of her voice caused the big cat to stir. Opening his eyes, he stared back at Jo. The sound he made was more grumble than roar before he dozed again. "He's tired," Jo murmured, fighting a shaft of gloom. "Twenty-two's old for a lion."

"What is it?" Keane demanded, touching her shoulder before she could turn away. Her eyes were drenched with sadness.

"He's dying," she said unsteadily. "And I can't stop it." Stuffing her hands in her pockets, Jo moved away to the main group of cages. To steady herself, she took two deep breaths while waiting for Keane to join her. Regaining her composure, she began again. "I work with these twelve," she told him, making a sweeping gesture. "They're fed once a day, raw meat six days a week and eggs and milk on the seventh. They were all imported directly from Africa and were cage broken when I got them."

The faint sound of a calliope reached them, signaling the opening of the midway. "This is Merlin, the one I ride out on at the finish. He's ten, and the most even-tempered cat I've ever worked with. Heathcliff," she continued as she moved down the line of cages, "he's six, my best leaper. And this is Faust, the baby at four and a half." The lions paced their cages as Jo walked Keane down the line. Unable to prevent herself, Jo gave Faust a signal by raising her hand. Obediently, he sent out a huge, deafening roar. To Jo's disappointment, Keane did not scramble for cover.

"Very impressive," he said mildly. "You put him in the center when you lie down on them, don't you?"

"Yes." She frowned, then spoke her thoughts candidly. "You're very observant—and you've got steady nerves."

"My profession requires them, too, to an extent," he returned.

Jo considered this a moment, then turned back to the lions. "Lazareth, he's twelve and a natural ham. Bolingbroke, he's ten, from the same lioness as Merlin. Hamlet," she said stopping again, "he's five. I bought him to replace Ari in the act." Jo stared into the tawny eyes. "He has potential, but he's arrogant. Patient, too. He's just waiting for me to make a mistake."

"Why?" Keane glanced over at Jo. Her eyes were cool and steady on Hamlet's.

"So he can get a good clean swipe at me," she told him without altering her expression. "It's his first season in the big cage. Pandora," Jo continued, pointing out the females. "A very classy lady. She's six. Hester, at seven, my best all-around. And Portia; it's her first year, too. She's mostly a seat-warmer."

"Seat-warmer?"

"Just what it sounds like," Jo explained. "She hasn't mastered any complicated tricks yet. She evens out the act, does a few basics and warms the seat." Jo moved on. "Dulcinea, the prettiest of the ladies. Ophelia, who had a litter last year; and Abra, eight, a bit bad-tempered but a good balancer."

Hearing her name, the cat rose, stretched her long, golden body, then began to rub it against the bars of the cage. A deep sound rumbled in her throat. Jo scowled and jammed her hands into her pockets. "She likes you," she muttered.

"Oh?" Lifting a brow, Keane studied the three-hundred-pound Abra more carefully. "How do you know?"

"When a lion likes you, it does exactly what a house cat does. It rubs against you. Abra's rubbing against the bars because she can't get any closer."

"I see." Humor touched his mouth. "I must admit, I'm at a loss on how to return the compliment." He drew on his cigar, then regarded Jo through a haze of smoke. "Your choice of names is fascinating."

"I like to read," she stated, leaving it at that. "Is there anything else you'd like to know about the cats?" Jo was determined to keep their conversation on a professional level. His smile had reminded her all too clearly of their encounter the night before.

"Do you drug them before a performance?"

Fury sparked Jo's eyes. "Certainly not."

"Was that an unreasonable question?" Keane countered. He dropped his cigar to the ground, then crushed it out with his heel.

"Not for a first of mayer," Jo decided with a sigh. She tossed her hair carelessly behind her back. "Drugging is not only cruel, it's stupid. A drugged animal won't perform."

"You don't touch the lions with that whip," Keane commented. He watched the light breeze tease a few strands of her hair. "Why do you use it?"

"To get their attention and to keep the audience awake." She smiled reluctantly.

Keane took her arm. Instantly, Jo stiffened. "Let's walk," he suggested. He began to lead her away from the cages. Spotting several people roaming the back yard, Jo refrained from pulling away. The last thing she wanted was the story spreading that she was having a tiff with the owner. "How do you tame them?" he asked her.

"I don't. They're not tame, they're trained."
A tall blond woman walked by carrying a tiny
white poodle. "Merlin's hungry today," Jo called
out with a grin.

The woman bundled the dog closer to her
breast in mock alarm and began a rapid scolding
in French. Jo laughed, telling her in the same
language that Fifi was too tough a mouthful for
Merlin.

"Fifi can do a double somersault on the back
of a moving horse," Jo explained as they began
to walk again. "She's trained just as my cats are
trained, but she's also domesticated. The cats are
wild." Jo turned her face up to Keane's. The sun
cast a sheen over her hair and threw gold flecks
into her eyes. "A wild thing can never be tamed,
and anyone who tries is foolish. If you take
something wild and turn it into a pet, you've sto-
len its character, blanked out its spark. And still,
there's always an essence of the wild that can
come back to life. When a dog turns on his mas-
ter, it's ugly. When a lion turns, it's lethal." She
was beginning to become accustomed to his hand
on her arm, finding it easy to talk to him because
he listened. "A full-grown male stands three feet
at the shoulder and weighs over five hundred
pounds. One well-directed swipe can break a
man's neck, not to mention what teeth and claws
can do." Jo gave a smile and a shrug. "Those
aren't the virtues of a pet."

"Yet you go into a cage with twelve of them, armed with a whip?"

"The whip's window dressing." Jo discounted it with a gesture of her hand. "It would hardly be a defense against even one cat at full charge. A lion is a very tenacious enemy. A tiger is more bloodthirsty, but it normally strikes only once. If it misses, it takes it philosophically. A lion charges again and again. Do you know the line Byron wrote about a tiger's spring? 'Deadly, quick and crushing.'" Jo had completely forgotten her animosity and began to enjoy her walk and conversation with this handsome stranger. "It's a true description, but a lion is totally fearless when he charges, and stubborn. He's not the razzle-dazzle fighter the tiger is, just accurate. I'd bet on a lion against a tiger any day. And a man simply hasn't a prayer against one."

"Then how do you manage to stay in one piece?"

The calliope music was just a hint in the air now. Jo turned, noting with surprise that they had walked a good distance from camp. She could see the trailers and tents, hear occasional shouts and laughter, but she felt oddly separated from it all. She sat down cross-legged on the grass and plucked a blade. "I'm smarter than they are. At least I make them think so. And I dominate them, partly by a force of will. In training, you have to develop a rapport, a mutual respect, and if you're lucky, a certain affection. But you can't trust them to the point where you grow careless. And above all,'' she added, glancing over as he sat down beside her, ''you have to remember the basic rule of poker. Bluff.'' Jo grinned, leaning back on her elbows. ''Do you play poker?''

''I've been known to.'' Her hair trailed out along the grass, and he lifted a strand. ''Do you?''

''Sometimes. My assistant handler, Pete...'' Jo scanned the back yard, then smiled and pointed. ''There he is, by the second trailer, sitting with Mac Stevenson, the one with the fielder's cap. Pete organizes a game now and then.''

''Who's the little girl on stilts?''

''That's Mac's youngest, Katie. She wants to walk on them in the street parade. She's getting pretty good. There's Jamie,'' she said, then laughed as he did a pratfall and landed at Katie's wooden stilts.

''Rose's Jamie?'' Keane asked, watching the impromptu show in the back yard.

''If she has her way. He's currently dazzled by Carmen Gribalti. Carmen won't give Jamie the time of day. She bats her lashes at Vito, the wire walker. He bats his at everyone.''

''A complicated state of affairs,'' Keane commented. He twisted Jo's hair around his fingers. ''Romance seems to be very popular in circus life.''

''From what I read,'' she countered, ''it's popular everywhere.''

"Who dazzles you, Jovilette?" He gave her hair a tug to bring her face around to his.

Jo hadn't realized he was so close. She need do no more than sway for her mouth to touch his. Her eyes measured his while she waited for her pulse to calm. It was odd, she thought, that he had such an effect on her. With sudden clarity, she could smell the grass, a clean, sweet scent, and feel the sun. The sounds of the circus were muted in the background. She could hear birds call out with an occasional high-pitched trill. She remembered the taste of his mouth and wondered if it would be the same.

"I've been too busy to be dazzled," she replied. Her voice was steady, but her eyes were curious.

For the first time, Jo truly *wanted* to be kissed by a man. She wanted to feel again what she had felt the night before. She wanted to be held, not lightly as he had held her before, but close, with his arms tight around her. She wanted to renew the feeling of weightlessness. She had never experienced a strong physical desire, and for a moment she explored the sensation. There was a quiver in her stomach which was both pleasant and disturbing. Throughout her silent contemplations Keane watched her, intrigued by the intensity of her eyes.

"What are you thinking of?"

"I'm wondering why you make me feel so odd," she told him with simple frankness. He smiled, and she noticed that it grew in his eyes seconds before it grew on his mouth.

"Do I?" He appeared to enjoy the information. "Did you know your hair catches the sunlight?" Keane took a handful, letting it spill from between his fingers. "I've never seen another woman with hair like this. It's a temptation all in itself. In what way do I make you feel odd, Jovilette?" he asked as his eyes trailed back up to hers.

"I'm not sure yet." Jo found her voice husky. Abruptly, she decided it would not do to go on feeling odd or to go on wanting to be kissed by Keane Prescott. She scrambled up and brushed off the seat of her pants.

"Running away?" As Keane rose, Jo's head snapped up.

"I never run away from anything, Mr. Prescott." Ice sharpened her voice. She was annoyed that she had allowed herself to fall under his charm again. "I certainly won't run from a city-bred lawyer." Her words were laced with scorn. "Why don't you go back to Chicago and get someone thrown in jail?"

"I'm a defense attorney," Keane countered easily. "I get people out of jail."

"Fine. Go put a criminal back on the streets, then."

Keane laughed, bringing Jo's temper even closer to the surface. "That covers both sides of the issue, doesn't it? You dazzle me, Jovilette."

"Well, it's strictly unintentional." She took a step back from the amusement in his eyes. She would not tolerate him making fun of her. "You don't belong here," she blurted out. "You have no business here."

"On the contrary," he disagreed in a cool, untroubled voice. "I have every business here. I own this circus."

"Why?" she demanded, throwing out her hands as if to push his words aside. "Because it says so on a piece of paper? That's all lawyers understand, I imagine—pieces of paper with strange little words. Why did you come? To look us over and calculate the profit and loss? What's the liquidation value of a dream, Mr. Prescott? What price do you put on the human spirit? Look at it!" she demanded, swinging her arm to encompass the lot behind them. "You only see tents and a huddle of trailers. You can't possibly understand what it all means. But Frank understood. He loved it."

"I'm aware of that." Keane's voice was still calm but had taken on a thin edge of steel. Jo saw that his eyes had grown dark and guarded. "He also left it to me."

"I don't understand why." In frustration, Jo stuffed her hands in her pockets and turned away.

"Neither do I, I assure you, but the fact remains that he did."

"Not once in thirty years did you visit him."
Jo whirled back around. Her hair followed in a
passionate arch. "Not once."

"Quite true," Keane agreed. He stood with his
weight even on both legs and watched her. "Of
course, some might look at it differently. Not
once in thirty years did he visit me."

"Your mother left him and took you to Chicago—"

"I won't discuss my mother," Keane interrupted in a tone of clipped finality.

Jo bit off a retort, spinning away from him
again. Still she could not find the reins to her
control. "What are you going to do with it?" she
demanded.

"That's my business."

"Oh!" Jo spun back, then shut her eyes and
muttered in a language he failed to understand.
"Can you be so arrogant? Can you be so dispassionate?" Her lashes fluttered up, revealing eyes
dark with anger. "Do the lives of all those people mean nothing to you? Does Frank's dream
mean nothing? Haven't you enough money already without hurting people to get more? Greed
isn't something you inherited from Frank."

"I'll only be pushed so far," Keane warned.

"I'd push you all the way back to Chicago if I
could manage it," she snapped.

"I wondered how much of a temper there was
behind those sharp green eyes," Keane commented, watching her passion pour color into her

cheeks. "It appears it's a full-grown one." Jo
started to retort, but Keane cut her off. "Just
hold on a minute," he ordered. "With or without your approval, I own this circus. It might be
easier for you if you adjusted to that. Be quiet,"
he added when her mouth opened again. "Legally, I can do with my—" He hesitated a moment, then continued in a mordant tone.
"—inheritance as I choose. I have no obligation
or intention of justifying my decision to you."

Jo dug her nails into her palms to help keep her
voice from shaking. "I never knew I could grow
to dislike someone so quickly."

"Jovilette." Keane dipped his hands into his
pockets, then rocked back on his heels. "You
disliked me before you ever saw me."

"That's true," she replied evenly. "But I've
learned to dislike you in person in less than
twenty-four hours. I have a show to do," she
said, turning back toward the lot. Though he did
not follow, she felt his eyes on her until she
reached her trailer and closed the door behind
her.

Thirty minutes later Jamie sprang through the
back door of the Big Top. He was breathless after a lengthy routine and hooked one hand
through his purple suspenders as he took in gulps
of air. He spotted Jo standing beside the white
mare. Her eyes were dark and stormy, her shoulders set and rigid. Jamie recognized the signs.

Something or someone had put Jo in a temper, and she had barely ten minutes to work her way out of it before her cue.

He crossed to her and gave a tug on her hair. "Hey."

"Hello, Jamie." Jo struggled to keep her voice pleasant, but he heard the traces of emotion.

"Hello, Jo," he replied in precisely the same tone.

"Cut it out," she ordered before taking a few steps away. The mare followed docilely. Jo had been trying for some time to put her emotions back into some semblance of order. She was not succeeding.

"What happened?" Jamie asked from directly behind her.

"Nothing," Jo snapped, then hated herself for the short nastiness of the word.

Jamie persisted, knowing her too well to be offended. "Nothing is one of my favorite topics of conversation." He put his hands on her shoulders, ignoring her quick, bad-tempered jerk. "Let's talk about it."

"There's nothing to talk about."

"Exactly." He began massaging the tension in her shoulders with his white gloved hands.

"Oh, Jamie." His good-heartedness was irresistible. Sighing, she allowed herself to be soothed. "You're an idiot."

"I'm not here to be flattered."

"I had an argument with the owner." Jo let out a long breath and shut her eyes.

"What're you doing having arguments with the owner?"

"He infuriates me." Jo whirled around. Her cape whipped and snapped with the movement. "He shouldn't be here. If he were back in Chicago..."

"Hold it." With a slight shake of her shoulders, Jamie halted Jo's outburst. "You know better than to get yourself worked up like this right before a show. You can't afford to have your mind on anything but what you're doing when you're in that cage."

"I'll be all right," she mumbled.

"Jo." There was censure in his voice mixed with affection and exasperation.

Reluctantly, Jo brought her gaze up to his. It was impossible to resist the grave eyes in the brightly painted face. With something between a sigh and a moan, she dropped her forehead to his chest. "Jamie, he makes me so mad! He could ruin everything."

"Let's worry about it when the time comes," Jamie suggested, patting her hair.

"But he doesn't understand us. He doesn't understand anything."

"Well, then it's up to us to make him understand, isn't it?"

Jo looked up and wrinkled her nose. "You're so logical."

"Of course I am," he agreed and struck a pose. As he wiggled his orange eyebrows, Jo laughed. "Okay?" he asked, then picked up his prop bucket.

"Okay," she agreed and smiled.

"Good, 'cause there's my cue."

When he disappeared behind the flap, Jo leaned her cheek against the mare and nuzzled a moment. "I don't think I'm the one to make him understand, though."

I wish he'd never come, she added silently as she vaulted onto the mare's back. I wish I'd never noticed how his eyes are like Ari's and how nice his mouth is when he smiles, she thought. Jo ran the tip of her tongue gingerly over her lips. I wish he'd never kissed me. *Liar.* Her conscience spoke softly in her ear: *Admit it, you're glad he kissed you. You've never felt anything like that before, and no matter what, you're glad he kissed you last night. You even wanted him to kiss you again today.*

She forced her mind clear, taking deep, even breaths until she heard the ringmaster announce her. With a flick of her heels, she sent the mare sprinting into the tent.

It did not go well. The audience cheered her, oblivious to any problem, but Jo was aware that the routine was far from smooth. And the cats sensed her preoccupation. Again and again they tested her, and again and again Jo was forced to alter her timing to compensate. When the act was over, her head throbbed from the strain of concentration. Her hands were clammy as she turned Merlin over to Buck.

The big man came back to her after securing the cage. "What's the matter with you?" he demanded without preamble. By the underlying and very rare anger in his voice, Jo knew he had observed at least a portion of her act. Unlike the audience, Buck would note any deviation. "You go in the cage like that again, one of those cats is going to find out what you taste like."

"My timing was a little off, that's all." Jo fought against the trembling in her stomach and tried to sound casual.

"A little?" Buck glowered, looking formidable behind the mass of blond beard. "Who do you think you're fooling? I've been around these ugly cats since before you were born. When you go in the cage, you've got to take your brain in with you."

Only too aware that he was right, Jo conceded. "I know, Buck. You're right." With a weary hand she pushed back her hair. "It won't happen again. I guess I was tired and a little off-balance." She sent him an apologetic smile.

Buck frowned and shuffled. Never in his forty-five years had he managed to resist feminine smiles. "All right," he muttered, then sniffed and made his voice firm. "But you go take a nap right after the finale. No coffee. I don't want to see you around again until dinner time."

"Okay, Buck." Jo kept her voice humble, though she was tempted to grin. The weakness was going out of her legs, and the dull buzz of fear was fading from between her temples. Still she felt exhausted and agreeable to Buck's uncharacteristic tone of command. A nap, she decided as Buck drove Merlin away, was just what she needed, not to mention that it was as good a way as any to avoid Keane Prescott for the rest of the day. Shooing this thought aside, Jo decided to while away the time until the finale in casual conversation with Vito the wire walker.

Chapter Four

It rained for three days. It was a solid down-pour, not heavy but insistent. As the circus wound its way north, the rain followed. Never-theless, canvas men pitched the tents in soggy fields and muddy lots while straw was laid on the hippodrome track and performers scurried from trailers to tents under dripping umbrellas.

The lot near Waycross, Georgia, was scattered with puddles under a thick, gray sky. Jo could only be grateful that no evening show had been scheduled. By six, it was nearly dark, with a chill teasing the damp air. She hustled from the cook-house after an early supper. She would check on the cats, she decided, then closet herself in her trailer, draw the curtains against the rain and curl up with a book. Shivering, she concluded that the idea was inspired.

She carried no umbrella but sought question-able shelter under a gray rolled-brimmed hat and thin windbreaker. Keeping her head lowered, she jogged across the mud, skimming around or hopping over puddles. She hummed lightly, an-ticipating the simple pleasures of an idle eve-ning. Her humming ended in a muffled gasp as she ran into a solid object. Fingers wrapped around her upper arms. Even before she lifted her head, Jo knew it was Keane who held her. She recognized his touch. Through some clever maneuvering, she had managed to avoid being alone with him since they had walked together and looked back on the circus.

"Excuse me, Mr. Prescott. I'm afraid I wasn't looking where I was going."

"Perhaps the weather's dampened your radar, Jovilette." He made no move to release her. Annoyed, Jo was forced to hold her hat steady with one hand as she tilted her head to meet his eyes. Rain fell cool on her face.

"I don't know what you mean."

"Oh, I think you do," Keane countered. "There's not another soul around. You've been careful to keep yourself in a crowd for days."

Jo blinked rain from her lashes. She admitted ruefully that it had been foolish to suppose he wouldn't notice her ploy. She saw he carried no umbrella either, nor did he bother with a hat. His hair was darkened with rain, much the same color that one of her cats would be if caught in an unexpected shower. It was difficult, in the murky light, to clearly make out his features, but the rain could not disguise his mockery.

"That's an interesting observation, Mr. Prescott," Jo said coolly. "Now, if you don't mind, I'm getting wet." She was surprised when she remained in his hold after a strong attempt on her part to pull away. Frowning, she put both hands against his chest and pushed. She discovered that she had been wrong; under the lean frame was an amazing amount of strength. Infuriated that she had misjudged him and that she was out-matched, Jo raised her eyes again. "Let me go," she demanded between clenched teeth.

"No," Keane returned mildly. "I don't be-lieve I will."

Jo glared at him. "Mr. Prescott, I'm cold and wet and I'd like to go to my trailer. Now, what do you want?"

"First, I want you to stop calling me Mr. Pres-cott." Jo pouted but she kept silent. "Second, I'd like an hour of your time for going over a list of personnel." He paused. Through her wind-breaker Jo could feel his fingers unyielding on her arms.

"Is there anything else?" she demanded, try-ing to sound bored.

For a moment there was only the sound of rain drumming on the ground and splashing into puddles. "Yes," Keane said quietly. "I think I'll just get this out of my system."

Jo's instincts were swift but they were stand-ing too close for her to evade him. And he was quick. Her protest was muffled against his mouth. Her arms were pinioned to her sides as his locked around her. Jo had felt a man's body against her own before—working out with the tumblers, practicing with the equestrians—but never with such clarity as this. She was aware of Keane in every fiber of her being. His body was whipcord lean and hard, his arms holding the strength she had discounted the first time she had seen him. But more, it was his mouth that mystified her. Now it was not gentle or testing; it took and plundered and demanded more before she could withhold a response.

Jo forgot the rain, though it continued to fall against her face. She forgot the cold. The warmth spread from inside, where her blood flowed fast, as her body was molded to Keane's. She forgot herself, or the woman she had thought herself to be, and discovered another. When he lifted his mouth, Jo kept her eyes closed, savoring the lingering pleasures, inviting fresh ones.

"More?" he murmured as his hand trailed up, then down her spine. Heat raced after it. "Kissing can be a dangerous pastime, Jo." He lowered his mouth again, then nipped at her soft bottom lip. "But you know all about danger, don't you?" He kissed her hard, leaving her breathless. "How courageous are you without your cats?"

Suddenly her heart raced to her throat. Her legs became rubbery, and a tingle sprinted up her spine. Jo recognized the feeling. It was the way she felt when she experienced a close call with the cats. Reaction would set in after the door of the safety cage locked behind her and the crisis had passed. It was then that fear found her. She studied Keane's bold, amber eyes, and her mouth went dry. She shuddered.

"You're cold." His voice was abruptly brisk. "Small wonder. We'll go to my trailer and get you some coffee."

"No!" Jo's protest was sharp and instantaneous. She knew she was vulnerable and she knew as well that she did not yet possess the experience to fight him. To be alone with him now was too great a risk.

Keane drew her away, but his grip remained firm. She could not read his expression as he searched her face. "What happened just now was personal," he told her. "Strictly man to woman. I'm of the opinion that love making should be personal. You're an appealing armful, Jovilette, and I'm accustomed to taking what I want, one way or another."

His words were like a shot of adrenaline. Jo's chin thrust forward, and her eyes flamed. "No one *takes* me, one way or another." She spoke with the deadly calm of fury. "If I make love with anyone, it's only because I want to."

"Of course," Keane agreed with an easy nod. "We're both aware you'll be willing when the time comes. We could make love quite successfully tonight, but I think it best if we know each other better first."

Jo's mouth trembled open and closed twice before she could speak. "Of all the arrogant, outrageous . . ."

"Truthful," Keane supplied, tossing her into incoherency again. "But for now, we have business, and while I don't mind kissing in the rain, I prefer to conduct business in a drier climate." He held up a hand as Jo started to protest. "I told you, the kiss was between a man and a woman. The business we have now is between the owner of this circus and a performer under contract. Understood?"

Jo took a long, deep breath to bring her voice to a normal level. "Understood," she agreed. Without another word she let him lead her across the slippery lot.

When they reached Keane's trailer, he hustled Jo inside without preliminaries. She blinked against the change in light when he hit the wall switch. "Take off your coat," he said briskly, pulling down her zipper before she could perform the task for herself. Instinctively, her hand reached for it as she took a step backward. Keane merely lifted a brow, then stripped off his own jacket. "I'll get the coffee." He moved down the length of the narrow trailer and disappeared around the corner where the tiny kitchen was set.

Slowly, Jo pulled off her dripping hat, letting her hair tumble free from where it had been piled under its confinement. With automatic movements she hung both her hat and coat on the hooks by the trailer door. It had been almost six months since she had stood in Frank's trailer, and like a woman visiting an old friend, she searched for changes.

The same faded lampshade adorned the maple table lamp that Frank had used for reading. The shade sat straight now, however, not at its usual slightly askew angle. The pillow that Lillie from wardrobe had sewn for him on some long-ago Christmas still sat over the small burn hole in the seat cushion of the couch. Jo doubted that Keane knew of the hole's existence. Frank's pipe stand sat, as always, on the counter by the side window. Unable to resist, Jo crossed over to run her finger over the worn bowl of his favorite pipe.

"Never could pack it right," she murmured to his well-loved ghost. Abruptly, her senses quivered. She twisted her head to see Keane watching her. Jo dropped her hand. A rare blush mantled her cheeks as she found herself caught unguarded.

"How do you take your coffee, Jo?"

She swallowed. "Black," she told him, aware that he was granting her the privacy of her thoughts. "Just black. Thank you."

Keane nodded, then turned to pick up two steaming mugs. "Come, sit down." He moved toward the Formica table that sat directly across from the kitchen. "You'd better take off your shoes. They're wet."

After squeaking her way down the length of the trailer, Jo sat down and pulled at the damp laces. Keane set both mugs on the table before disappearing into the back of the trailer. When he returned, Jo was already sipping at the coffee.

"Here." He offered her a pair of socks.

Surprised, Jo shook her head. "No, that's all right. I don't need . . ."

Her polite refusal trailed off as he knelt at her feet. "Your feet are like ice," he commented after cupping them in his palms. Briskly, he rubbed them while Jo sat mute, oddly disarmed by the gesture. The warmth was spreading dangerously past her ankles. "Since I'm responsible for keeping you out in the rain," he went on as he slipped a sock over her foot, "I'd best see to it you don't cough and sneeze your way through tomorrow's show. Such small feet," he murmured, running his thumb over the curve of her ankle as she stared wordlessly at the top of his head.

Raindrops still clung to and glistened in his hair. Jo found herself longing to brush them away and feel the texture of his hair beneath her fingers. She was sharply aware of him and wondered if it would always be this way when she was near him. Keane pulled on the second sock. His fingers lingered on her calf as he lifted his eyes. Hers were darkened with confusion as they met his. The body over which she had always held supreme control was journeying into frontiers her mind had not yet explored.

"Still cold?" Keane asked softly.

Jo moistened her lips and shook her head. "No. No, I'm fine."

He smiled a lazy, masculine smile that said as clearly as words that he was aware of his effect on her. His eyes told her he enjoyed it. Unsmiling, Jo watched him rise to his feet.

"It doesn't mean you'll win," she said aloud in response to their silent communication.

"No, it doesn't." Keane's smile remained as his gaze roamed possessively over her face. "That only makes it more interesting. Open and shut cases are invariably boring, hardly worth the trouble of going on if you've won before you've finished your opening statement."

Jo lifted her coffee and sipped, taking a moment to settle her nerves. "Are we here to discuss the law or circus business, counselor?" she asked, letting her eyes drift to his again as she set the mug back on the table. "If it's law, I'm afraid I'm going to disappoint you. I don't know much about it."

"What do you know about, Jovilette?" Keane slid into the chair beside hers.

"Cats," she said. "And Prescott's Circus Colossus. I'll be glad to let you know whatever I can about either."

"Tell me about you," he countered, and leaning back, pulled a cigar from his pocket.

"Mr. Prescott—" Jo began.

"Keane," he interrupted, flicking on his lighter. He glanced at the tip of his cigar, then back up at her through the thin haze of smoke.

"I was under the impression you wanted to be briefed on the personnel."

"You are a member of this circus, are you not?" Casually, Keane blew smoke at the ceiling. "I have every intention of being briefed on the entire troupe and see no reason why you shouldn't start with yourself." His eyes traveled back to hers. "Humor me."

Jo decided to take the line of least resistance. "It's a short enough story," she said with a shrug. "I've been with the circus all my life. When I was old enough, I started work as a generally useful."

"A what?" Keane paused in the action of reaching for the coffeepot.

"Generally useful," Jo repeated, letting him freshen her cup. "It's a circus term that means exactly what it says. Rose's parents, for instance, are generally usefuls. We get a lot of drifters who work that way, too. It's also written into every performer's contract, after the specific terms, that they make themselves generally useful. There isn't room in most circuses, and certainly not in a tent circus, for performers with star complexes. You do what's necessary, what's needed. Buck, my handler, fills in during a slump at the sideshow, and he's one of the best canvas men around. Pete is the best mechanic in the troupe. Jamie knows as much about lighting as most shandies—electricians," she supplied as Keane lifted a brow. "He's also a better-than-average tumbler."

"What about you?" Keane interrupted the flow of Jo's words. For a moment she faltered, and the hands that had been gesturing became still. "Besides riding a galloping horse without reins or saddle, giving orders to elephants and facing lions?" He lifted his cup, watching her as he sipped. A smile lurked in his eyes. Jo frowned, studying him.

"Are you making fun of me?"

His smile sobered instantly. "No, Jo, I'm not making fun of you."

She continued. "In a pinch, I run the menagerie in the sideshow or I fill in the aerial act. Not the trap," she explained, relaxing again. "They have to practice together constantly to keep the timing. But sometimes I fill in on the Spanish Web, the big costume number where the girls hang from ropes and do identical moves. They're using butterfly costumes this year."

"Yes, I know the one." Keane continued to watch her as he drew on his cigar.

"But mostly Duffy likes to use girls who are more curvy. They double as showgirls in the finale."

"I see." A smile tugged at the corners of Keane's mouth. "Tell me, were your parents European?"

"No." Diverted, Jo shook her head. "Why do you ask?"

"Your name. And the ease with which I've heard you speak both French and Italian."

"It's easy to pick up languages in the circus," Jo said.

"Your accent was perfect in both cases."

"What? Oh." She shrugged and absently shifted in her chair, bringing her feet up to sit cross-legged. "We have a wide variety of nationalities here. Frank used to say that the world could take a lesson from the circus. We have French, Italian, Spanish, German, Russian, Mexican, Americans from all parts of the country and more."

"I know. It's like a traveling United Nations." He tipped his cigar ash in a glass tray. "So you picked up some French and Italian along the way. But if you've traveled with the circus all your life, what about the rest of your schooling?"

The hint of censure in his voice brought up her chin. "I went to school during the winter break and had a tutor on the road. I learned my ABC's, counselor, and a bit more, besides. I probably know more about geography and world history than you, and from more interesting sources than textbooks. I imagine I know more about animals than a third-year veterinary student and have more practical experience healing them. I can speak seven languages and—"

"Seven?" Keane interrupted. "Seven languages?"

"Well, five fluently," she corrected grudgingly. "I still have a bit of trouble with Greek and German, unless I can really take my time, and I can't read Greek yet at all."

"What else besides French, Italian and English?"

"Spanish and Russian." Jo scowled into her coffee. "The Russian's handy. I use it for swearing at the cats during the act. Not too many people understand Russian cursing, so it's safe."

Keane's laughter brought Jo's attention from her coffee. He was leaning back in his chair, his eyes gold with their mirth. Jo's scowl deepened. "What's so funny?"

"You are, Jovilette." Stung, she started to scramble up, but his hands on her shoulders stopped her. "No, don't be offended. I can't help but find it amusing that you toss out so offhandedly an accomplishment that any language major would brag about." Carelessly, he ran a finger over her sulky mouth. "You continually amaze me." He brushed a hand through her hair. "You mumbled something at me the other day. Were you swearing at me in Russian?"

"Probably."

Grinning, Keane dropped his hand and settled into his chair again. "When did you start working with the cats?"

"In front of an audience? When I was seventeen. Frank wouldn't let me start any earlier. He was my legal guardian as well as the owner, so he

had me both ways. I was ready when I was fifteen."

"How did you lose your parents?"

The question caught her off guard. "In a fire,"
she said levelly. "When I was seven."

"Here?"

She knew Keane was not referring to their lo-
cale but to the circus. Jo sipped her cooling coffee. "Yes."

"Didn't you have any other family?"

"The circus is a family," she countered. "I was
never given the chance to be an orphan. And I
always had Frank."

"Did you?" Keane's smile was faintly sarcas-
tic. "How was he as a father figure?"

Jo studied him for a moment. Was he bitter?
she wondered. Or amused? Or simply curious?
"He never took my father's place," she replied
quietly. "He never tried to, because neither of us
wanted it. We were friends, as close as I think it's
possible for friends to be, but I'd already had a
father, and he'd already had a child. We weren't
looking for substitutes. You look nothing like
him, you know."

"No," Keane replied with a shrug. "I know."

"He had a comfortable face, all creases and
folds." Jo smiled, thinking of it while she ran a
finger absently around the rim of her mug. "He
was dark, too, just beginning to gray when . . ."
She trailed off, then brought herself back with a
quick shake of her head. "Your voice is rather

like his, though; he had a truly beautiful voice. I'll ask you a question now.''

Keane's expression became attentive, then he gestured with the back of his hand. ''Go ahead.''

''Why are you here? I lost my temper when I asked you before, but I do want to know.'' It was against her nature to probe, and some of her discomfort found its way into her voice. ''It must have caused you some difficulty to leave your practice, even for a few weeks.''

Keane frowned at the end of his cigar before he slowly crushed it out. ''Let's say I wanted to see firsthand what had fascinated my father all these years.''

''You never came when he was alive.'' Jo gripped her hands together under the table. ''You didn't even bother to come to his funeral.''

''I would've been the worst kind of hypocrite to attend his funeral, don't you think?''

''He was your father.'' Jo's eyes grew dark and her tone sharp in reproof.

''You're smarter than that, Jo,'' Keane countered calmly. ''It takes more than an accident of birth to make a father. Frank Prescott was a complete stranger to me.''

''You resent him.'' Jo felt suddenly torn between loyalty for Frank and understanding for the man who sat beside her.

''No.'' Keane shook his head thoughtfully. ''No, I believe I actively resented him when I was growing up, but..." He shrugged the thought aside. "I grew rather ambivalent over the years."

"He was a good man," Jo stated, leaning forward as she willed him to understand. "He only wanted to give people pleasure, to show them a little magic. Maybe he wasn't made to be a father—some men aren't—but he was kind and gentle. And he was proud of you."

"Of me?" Keane seemed amused. "How?"

"Oh, you're hateful," Jo whispered, hurt by his careless attitude. She slipped from her chair, but before she could step away, Keane took her arm.

"No, tell me. I'm interested." His hold on her arm was light, but she knew it would tighten if she resisted.

"All right." Jo tossed her head to send her hair behind her back. "He had the Chicago paper delivered to his Florida office. He always looked for any mention of you, any article on a court case you were involved in or a dinner party you attended. Anything. You have to understand that to us a write-up is very important. Frank wasn't a performer, but he was one of us. Sometimes he'd read me an article before he put it away. He kept a scrapbook."

Jo pulled her arm away and strode past Keane into the bedroom. The oversize wooden chest was where it had always been, at the foot of Frank's bed. Kneeling down, Jo tossed up the lid. "This is where he kept all the things that mattered to him." Jo began to shift through papers and mementos quickly; she had not been able to bring herself to sort through the chest before. Keane stood in the doorway and watched her. "He called it his memory box." She pushed at her hair with an annoyed hand, then continued to search. "He said memories were the rewards for growing old. Here it is." Jo pulled out a dark green scrapbook, then sat back on her heels. Silently, she held it out to Keane. After a moment he crossed the room and took it from her. Jo could hear the rain hissing on the ground outside as their eyes held. His expression was unfathomable as he opened the book. The pages rustled to join the quiet sound of the rain.

"What an odd man he must have been," Keane murmured, "to keep a scrapbook on a son he never knew." There was no rancor in his voice. "What was he?" he asked suddenly, shifting his eyes back to Jo.

"A dreamer," she answered. "His watch was always five minutes slow. If he hung a picture on the wall, it was always crooked. He'd never straighten it because he'd never notice. He was always thinking about tomorrow. I guess that's why he kept yesterday in this box." Glancing down, she began to straighten the chaos she had caused while looking for the book. A snatch of red caught her eye. Reaching for it, her fingers found a familiar shape. Jo hesitated, then drew the old doll out of the chest.

It was a sad piece of plastic and faded silk with its face nearly washed away. One arm was broken off, leaving an empty sleeve. The golden hair was straggled but brave under its red cap. Ballet shoes were painted on the dainty feet. Tears backed up behind Jo's eyes as she made a soft sound of joy and despair.

"What is it?" Keane demanded, glancing down to see her clutching the battered ballerina.

"Nothing." Her voice was unsteady as she scrambled quickly to her feet. "I have to go." Though she tried, Jo could not bring herself to drop the doll back into the box. She swallowed. She did not wish to reveal her emotions before his intelligent, gold eyes. Perhaps he would be cynical, or worse, amused. "May I have this, please?" She was careful with the tone of the request.

Slowly, Keane crossed the distance between them, then cradled her chin in his hand. "It appears to be yours already."

"It was." Her fingers tightened on the doll's waist. "I didn't know Frank had kept it. Please," she whispered. Her emotions were already dangerously heightened. She could feel a need to rest her head against his shoulder. The evening had been a roller coaster for her feelings, climaxing now with the discovery of her most prized childhood possession. She knew that if she did not escape, she would seek comfort in his arms. Her own weakness frightened her. "Let me by."

For a moment, Jo read refusal in his eyes. Then he stepped aside. Jo let out a quiet, shaky breath. "I'll walk you back to your trailer."

"No," she said quickly, too quickly. "It isn't necessary," she amended, moving by him and into the kitchen. Sitting down, she pulled on her shoes, too distraught to remember she still wore his socks. "There's no reason for us both to get wet again." She rambled on, knowing he was watching her hurried movement, but unable to stop. "And I'm going to check on my cats before I go in, and..."

She stopped short when he took her shoulders and pulled her to her feet. "And you don't want to take the chance of being alone in your trailer with me in case I change my mind."

A sharp denial trembled on her lips, but the knowledge in his eyes crushed it. "All right," she admitted. "That, too."

Keane brushed her hair from her neck and shook his head. He kissed her nose and moved down to pluck her hat and coat from their hooks. Cautiously, Jo followed him. When he held out her coat, she turned and slipped her arms into the sleeves. Before she could murmur her thanks, he turned her back and pulled up the zipper. For a moment his fingers lingered at her neck, his eyes on hers. Taking her hair into his hand, he piled it atop her head, then dropped on her hat. The gestures were innocent, but Jo was rocked by a feeling of intimacy she had never experienced.

"I'll see you tomorrow," he said, pulling the brim of her hat down further over her eyes.

Jo nodded. Holding the doll against her side, she pushed open the door. The sound of rain was amplified through the trailer. "Good night," she murmured, then moved quickly into the night.

Chapter Five

The morning scent was clean. In the new lot rainbows glistened in puddles. At last the sky was blue with only harmless white puffs of clouds floating over its surface. In the cookhouse a loud, crowded breakfast was being served. Finding herself without appetite, Jo skipped going to the cookhouse altogether. She was restless and tense. No matter how she disciplined her mind, her thoughts wandered back to Keane Prescott and to the evening they had spent together. Jo remembered it all, from the quick passion of the kiss in the rain to the calmness of his voice when he had said good-night. It was odd, she mused, that whenever she began to talk to him, she forgot he was the owner, forgot he was Frank's son. Always she was forced to remind herself of their positions.

Deep in thought, Jo slipped into tights and a leotard. It was true, she admitted, that she had failed to keep their relationship from becoming personal. She found it difficult to corral her urge to laugh with him, to share a joke, to open for him the doorway to the magic of the circus. If he could feel it, she thought, he would understand.

Though she could admit her interest in him privately, she could not find a clear reason for his apparent interest in her.

Why me? she wondered with a shake of her head. Turning, she opened her wardrobe closet and studied herself in the full-length glass on the back of the door. There she saw a woman of slightly less-than-average height with a body lacking the generous curves of Duffy's showgirls. The legs, she decided, were not bad. They were long and well-shaped with slim thighs. The hips were narrow, more, she thought with a pout, like a boy's than a woman's; and the bust line was sadly inadequate. She knew many women in the troupe with more appeal and a dozen with more experience.

Jo could see nothing in the mirror that would attract a sophisticated Chicago attorney. She did not note the honesty that shone from the exotically shaped green eyes or the strength in her chin or the full promise of her mouth. She saw the touch of gypsy in the tawny complexion and raven hair but remained unaware of the appeal that came from the hint of something wild and untamed just under the surface. The plain black leotard showed her firm, lithe body to perfection, but Jo thought nothing of the smooth satiny sheen of her skin. She was frowning as she pulled her hair back and began to braid it.

He must know dozens of women, she thought as her hands worked to confine her thick mane of hair. He probably takes a different one to dinner every night. They wear beautiful clothes and expensive perfume, she mused, torturing herself with the thought. They have names like Laura and Patricia, and they have low, sophisticated laughs. Jo lifted a brow at the reflection in the mirror and gave a light, low laugh. She wrinkled her brow at the hollowness of the sound. They discuss mutual friends, the Wallaces or the Jamesons, over candlelight and Beaujolais. And when he takes the most beautiful one home, they listen to Chopin and drink brandy in front of the fire. Then they make love. Jo felt an odd tightening in her stomach but pursued the fantasy to the finish. The lovely lady is experienced, passionate and worldly. Her skin is soft and white. When he leaves, she is not devastated but mature. She doesn't even care if he loves her or not.

Jo stared at the woman in the glass and saw her cheeks were wet. On a cry of frustration, she slammed the door shut. *What's wrong with me?* she demanded, brushing all traces of tears from her face. I haven't been myself for days! I need to shake myself out of this—this . . . whatever it is that I'm in. Slipping on gymnastic shoes and tossing a robe over her arm, Jo hustled from the trailer.

She moved carefully, avoiding puddles and any further speculation on Keane Prescott's romantic life. Before she was halfway across the lot, she saw Rose. From the expression on her face, Jo could see she was in a temper.

"Hello, Rose," she said, strategically stepping aside as the snake charmer splashed through a puddle.

"He's hopeless," Rose tossed back. "I tell you," she continued, stopping and wagging a finger at Jo, "I'm through this time. Why should I waste my time?"

"You've certainly been patient," Jo agreed, deciding that sympathy was the wisest course. "It's more than he deserves."

"Patient?" Rose raised a dramatic hand to her breast. "I have the patience of a saint. Yet even a saint has her limits!" Rose tossed her hair behind her shoulders. She sighed heavily. "*Adios.* I think I hear Mama calling me."

Jo continued her walk toward the Big Top. Jamie walked by, his hands in his pockets. "She's crazy," he muttered. He stopped and spread his arms wide. His look was that of a man ill-used and innocent. Jo shrugged. Shaking his head, Jamie moved away. "She's crazy," he said again.

Jo watched him until he was out of sight, then darted to the Big Top.

Inside, Carmen watched adoringly while Vito practiced a new routine on the incline wire. The tent echoed with the sounds of rehearsals: voices and thumps, the rattle of rigging, the yapping of clown dogs. In the first ring Jo spotted the Six Beirots, an acrobatic act that was just beginning its warm-ups. Pleased with her timing, Jo walked the length of the arena. A raucous whistle sounded over her head, and she glanced up to shake a friendly fist at Vito. He called from fifteen feet above her as he balanced on a slender wire set at a forty-five-degree angle.

"Hey, chickie, you have a nice rear view. You're almost as cute as me."

"No one's as cute as you, Vito," she called back.

"Ah, I know." With a weighty sigh, he executed a neat pivot. "But I have learned to live with it." He sent down a lewd wink. "When you going into town with me, chickie?" he asked as he always did.

"When you teach my cats to walk the wire," Jo answered as she always did. Vito laughed and began a light-footed cha-cha. Carmen fired Jo a glare. She must have it bad, Jo decided, if she takes Vito's harmless flirting seriously. Stopping beside her, Jo leaned close and spoke in a conspirator's whisper. "He'd fall off his wire if I said I'd go."

"I'd go," Carmen said with a lovely pout, "if he'd just ask me."

Jo shook her head, wondering why romances were invariably complicated. She was lucky not to have the problem. Giving Carmen an encouraging pat on the shoulder, Jo set off toward the first ring.

* * *

The Six Beirots were brothers. They were all small-statured, dark men who had immigrated from Belgium. Jo worked out with them often to keep herself limber and to keep her reflexes sharp. She liked them all, knew their wives and children, and understood their unique blending of French and English. Raoul was the oldest, and the stockiest of the six brothers. Because of his build and strength, he was the under-stander in their human pyramid. It was he who spotted Jo and first lifted a hand in greeting.

"Halo." He grinned and ran his palm over his receding hairline. "You gonna tumble?"

Jo laughed and did a quick handspring into the ring. She stuck out her tongue when the unanimous critique was "sloppy." "I just need to warm up," she said, assuming an air of injured dignity. "My muscles need tuning."

For the next thirty minutes Jo worked with them, doing muscle stretches and limbering exercises, rib stretches and lung expanders. Her muscles warmed and loosened, her heart pumped steadily. She was filled with energy. Her mind was clear. Because of her lightened mood, Jo was easily cajoled into a few impromptu acrobatics. Leaving the more complicated feats to the experts, she did simple back flips, handsprings or twists at Raoul's command. She did a brief, semi-successful thirty seconds atop the rolling globe and earned catcalls from her comrades at her dismount.

She stood back as they began the leaps. One after another they lined up to take turns running along a ramp, bounding upon a springboard and flying up to do flips or twists before landing on the mat. There was a constant stream of French as they called out to each other.

"Hokay, Jo." Raoul gestured with his hand. "Your turn."

"Oh, no." She shook her head and reached for her robe. "Uh-uh." There was a chorus of coaxing, teasing French. "I've got to give my cats their vitamins," she told them, still shaking her head.

"Come on, Jo. It's fun." Raoul grinned and wiggled his eyebrows. "Don't you like to fly?" As she glanced at the ramp, Raoul knew she was tempted. "You take a good spring," he told her. "Do one forward somersault, then land on my shoulders." He patted them to show their ability to handle the job.

Jo smiled and nibbled pensively on her lower lip. It had been a long while since she had taken the time to go up on the trapeze and really fly. It did look like fun. She gave Raoul a stern look. "You'll catch me?"

"Raoul never misses," he said proudly, then turned to his brothers. *"Ne c'est pas?"* His brothers shrugged and rolled their eyes to the ceiling with indistinguishable mutters. "Ah." He waved them away with the back of his hand.

Knowing Raoul was indeed a top flight understander, Jo approached the ramp. Still she gave him one last narrow-eyed look. "You catch me," she ordered, shaking her finger at him.

"Cherie." He took his position with a stylish movement of his hand. "It's a piece of pie."

"Cake," Jo corrected, took a deep breath, held it and ran. When she came off the springboard, she tucked into the somersault and watched the Big Top turn upside down. She felt good. As the tent began to right itself, she straightened for her landing, keeping herself loose. Her feet connected with Raoul's powerful shoulders, and she tilted only briefly before he took her ankles in a firm grip. Straightening her poor posture, Jo styled elaborately with both arms while she received exaggerated applause and whistles. She leaped down nimbly as Raoul took her waist to give her landing bounce.

"When do you want to join the act?" he asked her, giving her a friendly pat on the bottom. "We'll put you up on the sway pole."

"That's okay." Grinning, Jo again reached for her robe. "I'll stick with the cats." After a cheerful wave, she slipped one arm into a sleeve and started back down the hippodrome track. She pulled up short when she spotted Keane leaning up against the front seat rail.

"Amazing," he said, then straightened to move to her. "But then, the circus is supposed to be amazing, isn't it?" He lifted the forgotten sleeve to her robe, then slipped her other arm into it. "Is there anything here you can't do?"

"Hundreds of things," Jo answered, taking him seriously. "I'm only really proficient with animals. The rest is just show and play."

"You looked amazingly proficient to me for the last half hour or so," he countered as he pulled out her braid from where it was trapped by her robe.

"Have you been here that long?"

"I walked in as Vito was commenting on your rear view."

"Oh." Jo laughed, glancing back to where Vito now stood flirting with Carmen. "He's crazy."

"Perhaps," Keane agreed, taking her arm. "But his eyesight's good enough. Would you like some coffee?"

Jo was reminded instantly of the evening before. Leery of being drawn to his charms again, she shook her head. "I've got to change," she told him, belting her robe. "We've got a show at two. I want to rehearse the cats."

"It's incredible how much time you people devote to your art. Rehearsals seem to run into the beginning of a show, and a show seems to run into more rehearsals."

Jo softened when he referred to circus skills as art. "Performers always look for just a bit more in themselves. It's a constant struggle for perfection. Even when a performance goes beautifully and you know it, you start thinking about the next time. How can I do it better or bigger or higher or faster?''

"Never satisfied?" Keane asked as they stepped out into the sunlight.

"If we were, we wouldn't have much of a reason to come back and do it all over again."

He nodded, but there was something absent in the gesture, as if his mind was elsewhere. "I have to leave this afternoon," he said almost to himself.

"Leave?" Jo's heart skidded to a stop. Her distress was overwhelming and so unexpected that she was forced to take an extra moment to steady herself. "Back to Chicago?"

"*Hmm?*" Keane stopped, turning to face her. "Oh, yes."

"And the circus?" Jo asked, thoroughly ashamed that it had not been her first concern. She didn't want him to leave, she suddenly realized.

Keane frowned a moment, then continued to walk. "I see no purpose in disrupting this year's schedule." His voice was brisk now and businesslike.

"This year's?" Jo repeated cautiously.

Keane turned and looked at her. "I haven't decided its ultimate fate, but I won't do anything until the end of the summer."

"I see." She let out a long breath. "So we have a reprieve."

"In a manner of speaking," Keane agreed.

Jo was silent for a moment but could not prevent herself from asking, "Then you won't—I mean, you'll be staying in Chicago now; you won't be traveling with us?"

They negotiated their way around a puddle before Keane answered. "I don't feel I can make a judicious decision about the circus after so brief an exposure. There's a complication in one of my cases that needs my personal attention, but I should be back in a week or two."

Relief flooded through her. He would be back, a voice shouted in her ear. It shouldn't matter to you, another whispered. "We'll be in South Carolina in a couple of weeks," Jo said casually. They had reached her trailer, and she took the handle of her door before she turned to face him. *It's just that I want him to understand what this circus means,* she told herself as she looked up into his eyes. *That's the only reason I want him to come back.* Knowing she was lying to herself made it difficult to keep her gaze steady.

Keane smiled, letting his eyes travel over her face. "Yes, Duffy's given me a route list. I'll find you. Aren't you going to ask me in?"

"In?" Jo repeated. "Oh, no, I told you, I have to change, and..." He stepped forward as she talked. Something in his eyes told her a firm stand was necessary. She had seen a similar look in a lion's eyes while he contemplated taking a dangerous liberty. "I simply don't have time right now. If I don't see you before you go, have a good trip." She turned and opened the door. Aware of a movement, she turned back, but not before he had nudged her through the door and followed. As it closed at his back, Jo bristled with fury. She did not enjoy being outmaneuvered. "Tell me, counselor, do you know anything about a law concerning breaking and entering?"

"Doesn't apply," he returned smoothly. "There was no lock involved." He glanced around at the attractive simplicity of Jo's trailer. The colors were restful earth tones without frills. The beige- and brown-flecked linoleum floor was spotlessly clean. It was the same basic floorplan as Frank's trailer, but here there were softer touches. There were curtains rather than shades at the windows; large, comfortable pillows tossed onto a forest green sofa; a spray of fresh wildflowers tucked into a thin, glass vase. Without comment Keane wandered to a black lacquer trunk that sat directly opposite the door. On it was a book that he picked up while Jo fumed. *"The Count of Monte Cristo,"* he read aloud and flipped it open. "In French," he stated, lifting a brow.

"It was written in French," Jo muttered, pulling it from his hand. "So I read it in French." Annoyed, she lifted the lid on the trunk, preparing to drop the book inside and out of his reach.

"Good heavens, are those all yours?" Keane stopped the lid on its downswing, then pushed books around with his other hand. "Tolstoy, Cervantes, Voltaire, Steinbeck. When do you have time in this crazy, twenty-four-hour world you live in to read this stuff?"

"I make time," Jo snapped as her eyes sparked. "My *own* time. Just because you're the owner doesn't mean you can barge in here and poke through my things and demand an account of my time. This is my trailer. I own everything in it."

"Hold on." Keane halted her rushing stream of words. "I wasn't demanding an account of your time, I was simply astonished that you could find enough of it to do this type of reading. Since I can't claim to be an expert on your work, it would be remarkably foolish of me to criticize the amount of time you spend on it. Secondly," he said, taking a step toward her—and though Jo stiffened in anticipation, he did not touch her— "I apologize for 'poking through your things,' as you put it. I was interested for several reasons. One being I have quite an extensive library myself. It seems we have a common interest, whether we like it or not. As for barging into your trailer, I can only plead guilty. If you choose to prosecute, I can recommend a couple of lousy attorneys who overcharge."

His last comment forced a smile onto Jo's reluctant lips. "I'll give it some thought." With more care than she had originally intended, Jo lowered the lid of the trunk. She was reminded that she had not been gracious. "I'm sorry," she said as she turned back to him.

His eyes reflected curiosity. "What for?"

"For snapping at you." She lifted her shoulders, then let them fall. "I thought you were criticizing me. I suppose I'm too sensitive."

Several seconds passed before he spoke. "Unnecessary apology accepted if you answer one question."

Mystified, Jo frowned at him. "What question?"

"Is the Tolstoy in Russian?"

Jo laughed, pushing loose strands of hair from her face. "Yes, it is."

Keane smiled, enjoying the two tiny dimples that flickered in her cheeks when she laughed. "Did you know that though you're lovely in any case, you grow even more so when you smile?"

Jo's laughter stilled. She was unaccustomed to this sort of compliment and studied him without any idea of how to respond. It occurred to her that any of the sophisticated women she had imagined that morning would have known precisely what to say. She would have been able to smile or laugh as she tossed back the appropriate comment. That woman, Jo admitted, was not Jovilette Wilder. Gravely, she kept her eyes on his. "I don't know how to flirt," she said simply.

Keane tilted his head, and an expression came and went in his eyes before she could analyze it. He stepped toward her. "I wasn't flirting with you, Jo, I was making an observation. Hasn't anyone ever told you that you're beautiful?"

He was much too close now, but in the narrow confines of the trailer, Jo had little room to maneuver. She was forced to tilt back her head to keep her eyes level with his. "Not precisely the way you did." Quickly, she put her hand to his chest to keep the slight but important distance between them. She knew she was trapped, but that did not mean she was defeated.

Gently, Keane lifted her protesting hand, turning it palm up as he brought it to his lips. An involuntary breath rushed in and out of Jo's lungs. "Your hands are exquisite," he murmured, tracing the fine line of blue up the back. "Narrow-boned, long-fingered. And the palms show hard work. That makes them more interesting." He lifted his eyes from her hand to her face. "Like you."

Jo's voice had grown husky, but she could do nothing to alter it. "I don't know what I'm supposed to say when you tell me things like that." Beneath her robe her breasts rose and fell with her quickening heart. "I'd rather you didn't."

"Do you really?" Keane ran the back of his hand along her jaw line. "That's a pity, because the more I look at you, the more I find to say. You're a bewitching creature, Jovilette."

"I have to change," she said in the firmest voice she could muster. "You'll have to go."

"That's unfortunately true," he murmured, then cupped her chin. "Come, then, kiss me goodbye."

Jo stiffened. "I hardly think that's necessary...."

"You couldn't be more wrong," he told her as he lowered his mouth. "It's extremely necessary." In a light, teasing whisper, his lips met hers. His arms encircled her, bringing her closer with only the slightest pressure. "Kiss me back, Jo," he ordered softly. "Put your arms around me and kiss me back."

For a moment longer she resisted, but the lure of his mouth nibbling at hers was too strong. Letting instinct rule her will, Jo lifted her arms and circled his neck. Her mouth grew mobile under his, parting and offering. Her surrender seemed to lick the flames of his passion. The kiss grew urgent. His arms locked, crushing her against him. Her quiet moan was not of protest but of wonder. Her fingers found their way into his hair, tangling in its thickness as they urged him closer. She felt her robe loosen, then his hands trail up her rib cage. At his touch, she shivered, feeling her skin grow hot, then cold, then hot again in rapid succession.

When his hand took her breast, she shied, drawing in her breath quickly. "Steady," he murmured against her mouth. His hands stroked gently, coaxing her to relax again. He kissed the corners of her mouth, waiting until she quieted before he took her deep again. The thin leotard molded her body. It created no barrier against the warmth of his searching fingers. They moved slowly, lingering over the peak of her breast, exploring its softness, wandering to her waist, then tracing her hip and thigh.

No man had ever touched her so freely. Jo was helpless to stop him, helpless against her own growing need for him to touch her again. Was this the passion she had read of so often? The passion that drove men to war, to struggle against all reason, to risk everything? She felt she could understand it now. She clung to him as he taught her—as she learned—the demands of her own body. Her mouth grew hungrier for the taste of him. She was certain she remained in his arms while seasons flew by, while decades passed, while worlds were destroyed and built again.

But when he drew away, Jo saw the same sun spilling through her windows. Eternity had only been moments.

Unable to speak, she merely stared up at him. Her eyes were dark and aware, her cheeks flushed with desire. But somehow, though it still tingled from his, her mouth maintained a youthful innocence. Keane's eyes dropped to it as his hands loitered at the small of her back.

"It's difficult to believe I'm the first man to touch you," he murmured. His eyes roamed to hers. "And quite desperately arousing. Particularly when I find you've passion to match your looks. I think I'd like to make love with you in the daylight first so that I can watch that marvelous control of yours slip away layer by layer. We'll have to discuss it when I get back."

Jo forced strength back into her limbs, knowing she was on the brink of losing her will to him. "Just because I let you kiss me and touch me doesn't mean I'll let you make love to me." She lifted her chin, feeling her confidence surging back. "If I do, it'll be because it's what I want, not because you tell me to."

The expression in Keane's eyes altered. "Fair enough," he agreed and nodded. "It'll simply be my job to make it what you want." He took her chin in his hand and lowered his mouth to hers for a brief kiss. As she had the first time, Jo kept her eyes open and watched him. She felt him grin against her mouth before he raised his head. "You are the most fascinating woman I've ever met." Turning, he crossed to the door. "I'll be back," he said with a careless wave before it closed behind him. Dumbly, Jo stared into empty space.

Fascinating? she repeated, tracing her still warm lips with her fingertips. Quickly, she ran to the window, and kneeling on the sofa below it, watched Keane stride away.

She realized with a sudden jolt that she missed him already.

Chapter Six

Jo learned that weeks could drag like years. During the second week of Keane's absence she had searched each new lot for a sign of him. She had scanned the crowds of towners who came to watch the raising of the Big Top, and as the days stretched on and on, she balanced between anger and despair at his continued absence. Only in the cage did she manage to isolate her concentration, knowing she could not afford to do otherwise. But after each performance Jo found it more and more difficult to relax. Each morning she felt certain he would be back. Each night she lay restless, waiting for the sun to rise.

Spring was in full bloom. The high grass lots smelled of it. Often there were wildflowers crushed underfoot, leaving their heavy fragrances in the air. Even as the circus caravan traveled north, the days grew warm, sunlight lingering further into evening. While other troupers enjoyed the balmy air and providentially sunny skies, Jo lived on nerves.

It occurred to her that after returning to his life in Chicago, Keane had decided against coming back. In Chicago he had comfort and wealth and

elegant women. Why should he come back? Jo
closed her mind against the ultimate fate of the
circus, unwilling to face the possibility that Keane
might close the show at the end of the season. She
told herself the only reason she wanted him to
come back was to convince him to keep the circus open. But the memory of being in his arms
intruded too often into her thoughts. Gradually,
she grew resigned, filling the strange void she felt
with her work.

Several times each week she found time to give
the eager Gerry more training. At first she had
only permitted him to work with the two menagerie cubs, allowing him, with the protection of
leather gloves, to play with them and to feed
them. She encouraged him to teach them simple
tricks with the aid of small pieces of raw meat. Jo
was as pleased as he when the cats responded to
his patience and obeyed.

Jo saw potential in Gerry, in his genuine affection for animals and in his determination. Her
primary concern was that he had not yet devel-
oped a healthy fear. He was still too casual, and
with casualness, Jo knew, came carelessness.
When she thought he had progressed far enough,
Jo decided to take him to the next step of his
training.

There was no matinee that day, and the Big
Top was scattered with rehearsing troupers. Jo
was dressed in boots and khakis with a long-

sleeved blouse tucked into the waist. She studied Gerry as she ran the stock of her whip through her hand. They stood together in the safety cage while she issued instructions.

"All right, Buck's going to let Merlin through the chute. He's the most tractable of the cats, except for Ari." She paused a moment while her eyes grew sad. "Ari isn't up to even a short practice session." She pushed away the depression that threatened and continued. "Merlin knows you, he's familiar with your voice and your scent." Gerry nodded and swallowed. "When we go in, you're to be my shadow. You move when I move, and don't speak until I tell you. If you get frightened, don't run." Jo took his arm for emphasis. "That's *important,* understand? Don't run. Tell me if you want out, and I'll get you to the safety cage."

"I won't run, Jo," he promised and wiped hands, damp with excitement, on his jeans.

"Are you ready?"

Gerry grinned and nodded. "Yeah."

Jo opened the door leading to the big cage and let Gerry through behind her before securing it. She walked to the center of the arena in easy, confident strides. "Let him in, Buck," she called and heard the immediate rattle of bars. Merlin entered without hurry, then leaped onto his pedestal. He yawned hugely before looking at Jo. "A solo today, Merlin," she said as she advanced toward him. "And you're the star. Stay with me," she ordered as Gerry merely stood still and stared at the big cat. Merlin gave Gerry a disinterested glance and waited.

With an upward move of her arm, she sent Merlin into a sit-up. "You know," she told the boy behind her, "that teaching a cat to take his seat is the first trick. The audience won't even consider it one. The sit-up," she continued while signaling Merlin to bring his front paws back down, "is usually next and takes quite a bit of time. It's necessary to strengthen the cat's back muscles first." Again she signaled Merlin to sit up, then, with a quick command, she had him pawing the air and roaring. "Marvelous old ham," she said with a grin and brought him back down. "The primary move of each cue is always given from the same position with the same tone of voice. It takes patience and repetition. I'm going to bring him down off the pedestal now."

Jo flicked the whip against the tanbark, and Merlin leaped down. "Now I maneuver him to the spot in the arena where I want him to lie down." As she moved, Jo made certain her student moved with her. "The cage is a circle, forty feet in diameter. You have to know every inch of it inside your head. You have to know precisely how far you are from the bars at all times. If you back up into the bars, you've got no room to maneuver if there's trouble. It's one of the biggest mistakes a trainer can make." At her signal Merlin laid down, then shifted to his side. "Over,

Merlin," she said briskly, sending him into a series of rolls. "Use their names often; it keeps them in tune with you. You have to know each cat and their individual tendencies."

Jo moved with Merlin, then signaled him to stop. When he roared, she rubbed the top of his head with the stock of her whip. "They like to be petted just like house cats, but they are not tabbies. It's essential that you never give them your complete trust and that you remember always to maintain your dominance. You subjugate not by poking them or beating or shouting, which is not only cruel but makes for a mean, undependable cat, but with patience, respect and will. Never humiliate them; they have a right to their pride. You bluff them, Gerry," she said as she raised both arms and brought Merlin up on his hind legs. "Man is the unknown factor. That's why we use jungle-bred rather than captivity-bred cats. Ari is the exception. A cat born and raised in captivity is too familiar with man, so you lose your edge." She moved forward, keeping her arms raised. Merlin followed, walking on his hind legs. He spread seven feet into the air and towered over his trainer. "They might have a sense of affection for you, but there's no fear and little respect. Unfortunately, this often happens if a cat's been with a trainer a long time. They don't become more docile the longer they're in an act, but they become more dangerous. They test you constantly. The trick is to make them believe you're indestructible.''

She brought Merlin down, and he gave another yawn before she sent him back to his seat. ''If one swipes at you, you have to stop it then and there, because they try again and again, getting closer each time. Usually, if a trainer's hurt in the cage, it's because he's made a mistake. The cats are quick to spot them; sometimes they let them pass, sometimes they don't. This one's given me a good smack on the shoulder now and again. He's kept his claws retracted, but there's always the possibility that one time he'll forget he's just playing. Any questions?''

''Hundreds,'' Gerry answered, wiping his mouth with the back of his hand. ''I just can't focus on one right now.''

Jo chuckled and again scratched Merlin's head when he roared. ''They'll come to you later. It's hard to absorb anything the first time, but it'll come back to you when you're relaxed again. All right, you know the cue. Make him sit up.''

''Me?''

Jo stepped to the side, giving Merlin a clear view of her student. ''You can be as scared as you like,'' she said easily. ''Just don't let it show in your voice. Watch his eyes.''

Gerry rubbed his palm on the thighs of his jeans, then lifted it as he had seen Jo do hundreds of times. ''Up,'' he told the cat in a passably firm voice.

Merlin studied him a moment, then looked at Jo. This, his eyes told her clearly, was an amateur and beneath his notice. Carefully, Jo kept her face expressionless. "He's testing you," she told Gerry. "He's an old hand and a bit harder to bluff. Be firm and use his name this time."

Gerry took a deep breath and repeated the hand signal. "Up, Merlin."

Merlin glanced back at him, then stared with measuring, amber eyes. "Again," Jo instructed and heard Gerry swallow audibly. "Put some authority into your voice. He thinks you're a pushover."

"Up, Merlin!" Gerry repeated, annoyed enough by Jo's description to put some dominance into his voice. Though his reluctance was obvious, Merlin obeyed. "He did it," Gerry whispered on a long, shaky breath. "He really did it."

"Very good," Jo said, pleased with both the lion and her student. "Now bring him down." When this was accomplished, Jo had him bring Merlin from the seat. "Here." She handed Gerry the whip. "Use the stock to scratch his head. He likes it best just behind the ear." She felt the faint tremble in his hand as he took the whip, but he held it steady, even as Merlin closed his eyes and roared.

Because he had performed well, Jo afforded Merlin the liberty of rubbing against her legs before she called for Buck to let him out. The rattle of the bars was the cat's cue to exit, and like a trouper, he took it with his head held high. "You did very well," she told Gerry when they were alone in the cage.

"It was great." He handed her back the whip, the stock damp from his sweaty palms. "It was just great. When can I do it again?"

Jo smiled and patted his shoulder. "Soon," she promised. "Just remember the things I've told you and come to me when you remember all those questions."

"Okay, thanks, Jo." He stepped through the safety cage. "Thanks a lot. I want to go tell the guys."

"Go ahead." Jo watched him scramble away, leaping over the ring and darting through the back door. With a grin, she leaned against the bars. "Was I like that?" she asked Buck, who stood at the opposite end of the cage.

"The first time you got a cat to sit up on your own, we heard about it for a week. Twelve years old and you thought you were ready for the big show."

Jo laughed, and wiping the damp stock of her whip against her pants, turned. It was then she saw him standing behind her. "Keane!" she used the name she had sworn not to use as pleasure flooded through her. It shone on her face. Just as she had given up hope of seeing him again, he was there. She took two steps toward him before she could check herself. "I didn't know you were back." Jo gripped the stock of the whip with both hands to prevent herself from reaching out to touch him.

"I believe you missed me." His voice was as she remembered, low and smooth.

Jo cursed herself for being so naïve and transparent. "Perhaps I did, a little," she admitted cautiously. "I suppose I'd gotten used to you, and you were gone longer than you said you'd be." He looks the same, she thought rapidly, exactly the same. She reminded herself that it had only been a month. It had seemed like years.

"*Mmm,* yes. I had more to see to than I had expected. You look a bit pale," he observed and touched her cheek with his fingertip.

"I suppose I haven't been getting much sun," she said with quick prevarication. "How was Chicago?" Jo needed to turn the conversation away from personal lines until she had an opportunity to gauge her emotions; seeing him suddenly had tossed them into confusion.

"Cool," he told her, making a long, thorough survey of her face. "Have you ever been there?"

"No. We play near there toward the end of the season, but I've never had time to go all the way into the city."

Nodding absently, Keane glanced into the empty cage behind her. "I see you're training Gerry."

"Yes." Relieved that they had lapsed into a professional discussion, Jo let the muscles of her shoulders ease. "This was the first time with an adult cat and no bars between. He did very well."

Keane looked back at her. His eyes were serious and probing. "He was trembling. I could see it from where I stood watching you."

"It was his first time—" she began in Gerry's defense.

"I wasn't criticizing him," Keane interrupted with a tinge of impatience. "It's just that he stood beside you, shaking from head to foot, and you were totally cool and in complete control."

"It's my job to be in control," Jo reminded him.

"That lion must have stood seven feet tall when he went up on his hind legs, and you walked under him without any protection, not even the traditional chair."

"I do a picture act," she explained, "not a fighting act."

"Jo," he said so sharply she blinked. "Aren't you ever frightened in there?"

"Frightened?" she repeated, lifting a brow. "Of course I'm frightened. More frightened than Gerry was—or than you would be."

"What are you talking about?" Keane demanded. Jo noted with some curiosity that he was angry. "I could see that boy sweat in there."

"That was mostly excitement," Jo told him patiently. "He hasn't the experience to be truly frightened yet." She tossed back her hair and let out a long breath. Jo did not like to talk of her

fears with anyone and found it especially difficult with Keane. Only because she felt it necessary that he understand this to understand the
circus did she continue. "Real fear comes from
knowing them, working with them, understanding them. You can only speculate on what they
can do to a man. I *know*. I know exactly what
they're capable of. They have an incredible courage, but more, they have an incredible guile. I've
seen what they can do." Her eyes were calm and
clear as they looked into his. "My father almost
lost a leg once. I was about five, but I remember
it perfectly. He made a mistake, and a five-
hundred-pound Nubian sunk into his thigh and
dragged him around the arena. Luckily, the cat
was diverted by a female in season. Cats are un-
predictable when they have sex on their minds,
which is probably one of the reasons he attacked
my father in the first place. They're fiercely jealous once they've set their minds on a mate. My
father was able to get into the safety cage before
any of the other cats took an interest in him. I
can't remember how many stitches he had or how
long it was before he could walk properly again,
but I do remember the look in that cat's eyes.
You learn quickly about fear when you're in the
cage, but you control it, you channel it or you
find another line of work."

"Then why?" Keane demanded. He took her
shoulders before she could turn away. "Why do

you do it? And don't tell me because it's your job. That's not good enough.''

It puzzled Jo why he seemed angry. His eyes were darkened with temper, and his fingers dug into her shoulders. As if wanting to draw out her answer, he gave her one quick shake. ''All right,'' Jo said slowly, ignoring the ache in her flesh. ''That is part of it, but not all. It's all I've ever known, that's part of it, too. It's what I'm good at.'' While she spoke, she searched his face for a clue to his mood. She wondered if perhaps he had felt it wrong of her to take Gerry into the cage. ''Gerry's going to be good at it, too,'' she told him. ''I imagine everyone needs to be good— really good—at something. And I enjoy giving the people who come to see me the best show I can. But over all, I suppose it's because I love them. It's difficult for a layman to understand a trainer's feeling for his animals. I love their intelligence, their really awesome beauty, their strength, the unquenchable streak of wildness that separates them from well-trained horses. They're exciting, challenging and terrifying.''

Keane was silent for a moment. She saw that his eyes were still angry, but his fingers relaxed on her shoulders. Jo felt a light throbbing where bruises would certainly show in the morning. ''I suppose excitement becomes addicting—difficult to live without once it's become a habit.''

"I don't know," Jo replied, grateful that his temper was apparently cooling. "I've never thought about it."

"No, I suppose you'd have little reason to." With a nod, he turned to walk away.

Jo took a step after him. "Keane." His name raced through her lips before she could prevent it. When he turned back to her, she realized she could not ask any of the dozens of questions that flew through her mind. There was only one she felt she had any right to ask. "Have you thought any more about what you're going to do with us...with the circus?"

For an instant she saw temper flare again into his eyes. "No." The word was curt and final. As he turned his back on her again, she felt a spurt of anger and reached for his arm.

"How can you be so callous, so unfeeling?" she demanded. "How is it possible to be so casual when you hold the lives of over a hundred people in your hands?"

Carefully, he removed her hand from his arm. "Don't push me, Jo." There was warning in his eyes and in his voice.

"I'm not trying to," she returned, then ran a frustrated hand through her hair. "I'm only asking you to be fair, to be...kind," she finished lamely.

"Don't ask me anything," he ordered in a brisk, authoritative tone. Jo's chin rose in response. "I'm here," he reminded her. "You'll have to be satisfied with that for now."

Jo battled with her temper. She could not deny that in coming back he had proved himself true to his word. She had the rest of the season if nothing else. "I don't suppose I have any choice," she said quietly.

"No," he agreed with a faint nod. "You don't."

Frowning, Jo watched him stride away in a smooth, fluid gait she was forced to admire. She noticed for the first time that her palms were as damp as Gerry's had been. Annoyed, she rubbed them over her hips.

"Want to talk about it?"

Jo turned quickly to find Jamie behind her in full clown gear. She knew her preoccupation had been deep for her to be caught so completely unaware. "Oh, Jamie, I didn't see you."

"You haven't seen anything but Prescott since you stepped out of the cage," Jamie pointed out.

"What are you doing in makeup?" she asked, skirting his comment.

He gestured toward the dog at her feet. "This mutt won't respond to me unless I'm in my face. Do you want to talk about it?"

"Talk about what?"

"About Prescott, about the way you feel about him."

The dog sat patiently at Jamie's heels and thumped his tail. Casually, Jo stopped and ruffled his gray fur.

"I don't know what you're talking about."

"Look, I'm not saying it can't work out, but I don't want to see you get hurt. I know how it is to be nuts about somebody."

"What in the world makes you think I'm nuts about Keane Prescott?" Jo gave the dog her full attention.

"Hey, it's me, remember?" Jamie took her arm and pulled her to her feet. "Not everybody would've noticed, maybe, but not everybody knows you the way I do. You've been miserable since he went back to Chicago, looking for him in every car that drove on the lot. And just now, when you saw him, you lit up like the midway on Saturday night. I'm not saying there's anything wrong with you being in love with him, but—"

"In love with him?" Jo repeated, incredulous.

"Yeah." Jamie spoke patiently. "In love with him."

Jo stared at Jamie as the realization slid over her. "In love with him," she murmured, trying out the words. "Oh, no." She sighed, closing her eyes. "Oh, no."

"Didn't you have enough sense to figure it out for yourself?" Jamie said gently. Seeing Jo's distress, he ran a hand gently up her arm.

"No, I guess I'm pretty stupid about this sort of thing." Jo opened her eyes and looked around, wondering if the world should look any different. "What am I going to do?"

"Heck, I don't know." Jamie kicked sawdust with an oversized shoe. "I'm not exactly getting rave notices myself in that department." He gave Jo a reassuring pat. "I just wanted you to know that you always have a sympathetic ear here." He grinned engagingly before he turned to walk away, leaving Jo distracted and confused.

Jo spent the rest of the afternoon absorbed with the idea of being in love with Keane Prescott. For a short time she allowed herself to enjoy the sensation, the novel experience of loving someone not as a friend but as a lover. She could feel the light and the power spread through her, as if she had caught the sun in her hand. She daydreamed.

Keane was in love with her. He'd told her hundreds of times as he'd held her under a moonlit sky. He wanted to marry her, he couldn't bear to live without her. She was suddenly sophisticated and worldly enough to deal with the country club set on their own ground. She could exchange droll stories with the wives of other attorneys. There would be children and a house in the country. How would it feel to wake up in the same town every morning? She would learn to cook and give dinner parties. There would be long, quiet evenings when they would be alone together. There would be candlelight and music. When they slept together, his arms would stay around her until morning.

Idiot. Jo dragged herself back sternly. As she and Pete fed the cats, she tried to remember that fairy tales were for children. None of those things are ever going to happen, she reminded herself. I have to figure out how to handle this before I get in any deeper.

"Pete," she began, keeping her voice conversational as she put Abra's quota of raw meat on a long stick. "Have you ever been in love?"

Pete chewed his gum gently, watching Jo hoist the meat through the bars. "Well, now, let's see." Thrusting out his lower lip, he considered. "Only 'bout eight or ten times, I guess. Maybe twelve."

Jo laughed, moving down to the next cage. "I'm serious," she told him. "I mean *really* in love."

"I fall in love easy," Pete confessed gravely. "I'm a pushover for a pretty face. Matter of fact, I'm a pushover for an ugly face." He grinned. "Yes sir, the only thing like being in love is drawing an ace-high flush when the pot's ripe."

Jo shook her head and continued down the line. "Okay, since you're such an expert, tell me what you do when you're in love with a person and the person doesn't love you back and you don't want that person to know that you're in love because you don't want to make a fool of yourself.''

"Just a minute." Pete squeezed his eyes tight. "I got to think this one through first." For a moment he was silent as his lips moved with his thoughts. "Okay, let's see if I've got this straight." Opening his eyes, he frowned in concentration. "You're in love——"

"I didn't say *I* was in love," Jo interrupted hastily.

Pete lifted his brows and pursed his lips. "Let's just use *you* in the general sense to avoid confusion," he suggested. Jo nodded, pretending to absorb herself with the feeding of the cats. "So, you're in love, but the guy doesn't love you. First off, you've got to be sure he doesn't."

"He doesn't," Jo murmured, then added quickly, "let's say he doesn't."

Pete shot her a look out of the corner of his eye, then shifted his gum to the other side of his mouth. "Okay, then the first thing you should do is change his mind."

"Change his mind?" Jo repeated, frowning at him.

"Sure." Pete gestured with his hand to show the simplicity of the procedure. "You fall in love with him, then he falls in love with you. You play hard to get, or you play easy to get. Or you play flutter and smile." He demonstrated by coyly batting his lashes and giving a winsome smile. Jo giggled and leaned on the feeding pole. Pete in

fielder's cap, white T-shirt and faded jeans was
the best show she'd seen all day. "You make him
jealous," he continued. "Or you flatter his ego.
Girl, there're so many ways to get a man, I can't
count them, and I've been gotten by them all.
Yes, sir, I'm a real pushover." He looked so
pleased with his weakness, Jo smiled. How easy
it would be, she thought, if I could take love so
lightly.

"Suppose I don't want to do any of those
things. Suppose I don't really know how and I
don't want to humiliate myself by making a mess
of it. Suppose the person isn't—well, suppose
nothing could ever work between us, anyway.
What then?"

"You got too many supposes," Pete concluded, then shook his finger at her. "And I got
one for you. Suppose you ain't too smart because you figure you can't win even before you
play."

"Sometimes people get hurt when they play,"
Jo countered quietly. "Especially if they aren't
familiar with the game."

"Hurting's nothing," Pete stated with a sweep
of his hand. "Winning's the best, but playing's
just fine. This whole big life, it's a game, Jo. You
know that. And the rules keep changing all the
time. You've got nerve," he continued, then laid
his rough, brown hand on her shoulder. "More
raw nerve than most anybody I've ever known.
You've got brains, too, hungry brains. You go-

ing to tell me that with all that, you're afraid to take a chance?''

Meeting his eyes, Jo knew hypothetical evasions would not do. "I suppose I only take calculated risks, Pete. I know my turf; I know my moves. And I know exactly what'll happen if I make a mistake. I take a chance that my body might be clawed, not my emotions. I've never rehearsed for anything like this, and I think playing it cold would be suicide.''

"I think you've got to believe in Jo Wilder a little more,'' Pete countered, then gave her cheek a quick pat.

"Hey, Jo.'' Looking over, Jo saw Rose approaching. She wore straight-leg jeans, a white peasant blouse and a six-foot boa constrictor over her shoulders.

"Hello, Rose.'' Jo handed Pete the feeding pole. "Taking Baby out for a walk?''

"He needed some air.'' Rose gave her charge a pat. "I think he got a little carsick this morning. Does he look peaked to you?''

Jo looked down at the shiny, multicolored skin, then studied the tiny black eyes as Rose held Baby's head up for inspection. "I don't think so,'' she decided.

"Well, it's a warm day,'' Rose observed, releasing Baby's head. "I'll give him a bath. That might perk him up.''

Jo noticed Rose's eyes darting around the compound. "Looking for Jamie?''

"Hmph." Rose tossed her black curls. "I'm not wasting my time on that one." She stroked the latter half of Baby's anatomy. "I'm indifferent."

"That's another way to do it," Pete put in, giving Jo a nudge. "I forgot about that one. It's a zinger."

Rose frowned at Pete, then at Jo. "What's he talking about?"

With a laugh, Jo sat down on a water barrel. "Catching a man," she told her, letting the warm sun play on her face. "Pete's done a study on it from the male point of view."

"Oh." Rose threw Pete her most disdainful look. "You think I'm indifferent so he'll get interested?"

"It's a zinger," Pete repeated, adjusting his cap. "You get him confused so he starts thinking about you. You make him crazy wondering why you don't notice him."

Rose considered the idea. "Does it usually work?"

"It's got an eighty-seven percent success average," Pete assured her, then gave Baby a friendly pat. "It even works with cats." He jerked his thumb behind him and winked at Jo. "The pretty lady cat, she sits there and stares off into space like she's got important things occupying her mind. The boy in the next cage is doing everything but standing on his head to get her attention. She just gives herself a wash, pretending she doesn't even know he's there. Then, maybe after she's got him banging his head against the bars, she looks over, blinks her big yellow eyes and says, 'Oh, were you talking to me?'" Pete laughed and stretched his back muscles. "He's hooked then, brother, just like a fish on a line."

Rose smiled at the image of Jamie dangling from her own personal line. "Maybe I won't put Baby in Carmen's trailer after all," she murmured. "Oh, look, here comes Duffy and the owner." An inherent flirt, Rose instinctively fluffed her hair. "Really, he is the most handsome man. Don't you think so, Jo?"

Jo's eyes had already locked on Keane's. She seemed helpless to release herself from the gaze. Gripping the edge of the water barrel tightly, she reminded herself not to be a fool. "Yes," she agreed with studied casualness. "He's very attractive."

"Your knuckles are turning white, Jo," Pete muttered next to her ear.

Letting out a frustrated breath, Jo relaxed her hands. Straightening her spine, she determined to show more restraint. Control, she reminded herself, was the basic tool of her trade. If she could train her emotions and outbluff a dozen lions, she could certainly outbluff one man.

"Hello, Duffy." Rose gave the portly man a quick smile, then turned her attention to Keane. "Hello, Mr. Prescott. It's nice to have you back."

"Hello, Rose." He smiled into her upturned face, then lifted a brow as his eyes slid over the reptile around her neck and shoulders. "Who's your friend?"

"Oh, this is Baby." She patted one of the tan-colored saddle marks on Baby's back.

"Of course." Jo noticed how humor enhanced the gold of his eyes. "Hello, Pete." He gave the handler an easy nod before his gaze shifted and then lingered on Jo.

As on the first day they had met, Keane did not bother to camouflage his stare. His look was cool and assessing. He was reaffirming ownership. It shot through Jo that yes, she was in love with him, but she was also afraid of him. She feared his power over her, feared his capacity to hurt her. Still, her face registered none of her thoughts. Fear, she reminded herself as her eyes remained equally cool on his, was something she understood. Love might cause impossible problems, but fear could be dealt with. She would not cower from him, and she would honor the foremost rule of the arena. She would not turn and run.

Silently, they watched each other while the others looked on with varying degrees of curiosity. There was the barest touch of a smile on Keane's lips. The battle of wills continued until Duffy cleared his throat.

"Ah, Jo."

Calmly, without hurry, she shifted her attention. "Yes, Duffy?"

"I just sent one of the web girls into town to see the local dentist. Seems she's got an abscess. I need you to fill in tonight."

"Sure."

"Just for the web and the opening spectacular," he continued. Unable to prevent himself, he cast a quick look at Keane to see if he was still staring at her. He was. Duffy shifted uncomfortably and wondered what the devil was going on. "Take your usual place in the finale. We'll just be one girl shy in the chorus. Wardrobe'll fix you up."

"Okay." Jo smiled at him, though she was very much aware of Keane's eyes on her. "I guess I'd better go practice walking in those three-inch heels. What position do I take?"

"Number four rope."

"Duffy," Rose chimed in and tugged on his sleeve. "When are you going to let me do the web?"

"Rose, how's a pint-sizer like you going to stand up with that heavy costume on?" Duffy shook his head at her, keeping a respectable distance from Baby. After thirty-five years of working carnies, sideshows and circuses, he still was uneasy around snakes.

"I'm pretty strong," Rose claimed, stretching her spine in the hope of looking taller. "And I've been practicing." Anxious to demonstrate her accomplishments, Rose deftly unwound Baby. "Hold him a minute," she requested and dumped several feet of snake into Keane's arms.

"Ah . . ." Keane shifted the weight in his arms and looked dubiously into Baby's bored eyes. "I hope he's eaten recently."

"He had a nice breakfast," Rose assured him, going into a fluid backbend to show Duffy her flexibility.

"Baby won't eat owners," Jo told Keane. She did not bother to suppress her grin. It was the first time she had seen him disconcerted. "Just a stray towner, occasionally. Rose keeps him on a strict diet."

"I assume," Keane began as Baby slithered into a more comfortable position, "that he's aware I'm the owner."

Grinning at Keane's uncomfortable expression, Jo turned to Pete. "Gee, I don't know. Did anybody tell Baby about the new owner?"

"Haven't had a chance, myself," Pete drawled, taking out a fresh stick of gum. "Looks a lot like a towner, too. Baby might get confused."

"They're just teasing you, Mr. Prescott," Rose told him as she finished her impromptu audition with a full split. "Baby doesn't eat people at all. He's docile as a lamb. Little kids come up and pet him during a demonstration." She rose and brushed off her jeans. "Now, you take a cobra . . ."

"No, thank you," Keane declined, unloading the six-foot Baby back into Rose's arms.

Rose slipped the boa back around her neck. "Well, Duffy, I'm off. What do you say?"

"Get one of the girls to teach you the routine," he said with a nod. "Then we'll see." Smiling, he watched Rose saunter away.

"Hey, Duffy!" It was Jamie. "There's a couple of towners looking for you. I sent them over to the red wagon."

"Fine. I'll just go right on along with you." Duffy winked at Jo before turning to catch up with Jamie's long stride.

Keane was standing very close to the barrels. Jo knew getting down from her perch was risky. She knew, too, however, that her pulse was beginning to behave erratically despite her efforts to control it. "I've got to see about my costume." Nimbly, she came down, intending to skirt around him. Even as her boots touched the ground, his hands took her waist. Exercising every atom of willpower, she neither jerked nor struggled but lifted her eyes calmly to his.

His thumbs moved in a lazy arch. She could feel the warmth through the fabric of her blouse. With her entire being she wished he would not hold her. Then, perversely, she wished he would hold her closer. She struggled not to weaken as her lips grew warm under the kiss of his eyes. Her heart began to hammer in her ears.

Keane ran a hand down the length of her long, thick braid. Slowly, his eyes drifted back to hers. Abruptly, he released her and backed up to let her pass. "You'd best go have wardrobe take a few tucks in that costume."

Deciding she was not meant to decipher his changing moods, Jo stepped by him and crossed the compound. If she spent enough time working, she could keep her thoughts from dwelling on Keane Prescott. Maybe.

Chapter Seven

The Big Top was packed for the evening show. Jo watched the anticipation in the range of faces as she took her temporary position in the opening spectacular. The band played jumpy, upbeat music, leaning heavily on brass as the theme parade marched around the hippodrome track. As the substitute Bo Peep, Jo wore a demure mopcap and a wide crinoline skirt and led a baby lamb on a leash. Because her act came so swiftly on the tail of the opening, she rarely participated in the spectacular. Now she enjoyed a close-up look at the audience. In the cage, she blocked them out almost completely.

They were, she decided, a well-mixed group: young babies, older children, parents, grandparents, teen-agers. They gave the pageant enthusiastic applause. Jo smiled and waved as she performed the basic choreography with hardly a thought.

After a quick costume change, she took her cue as Queen of the Jungle Cats. After that followed another costume change that transformed her into one of the Twelve Spinning Butterflies.

"Just heard," Jamie whispered in her ear as she took the customary pose by the rope. "You got the job for the next week. Barbara won't be able to handle the teeth grip."

Jo shifted her shoulders to compensate for the weight of her enormous blue wings. "Rose is going to learn the routine," she mumbled back, smiling in the flood of the sunlight. "Duffy's giving her the job if she can stand up under this blasted costume." She made a quick, annoyed sound and smiled brightly. "It weighs a ton."

Slowly, to the beat of the waltz the band played, Jo climbed hand over hand up the rope. "Ah, show biz," she heard Jamie sigh. She vowed to poke him in the ribs when she took her bow. Then, hooking her foot in the hoop, she began the routine, imitating the other eleven Spinning Butterflies.

She was able to share a cup of coffee with Rose's mother when she returned the butterfly costume to wardrobe and changed into her own white and gold jumpsuit. Her muscles complained a bit due to the unfamiliar weight of the wings, and she gave a passing thought to a long, luxurious bath. That was a dream for September, she reminded herself. Showers were the order of the day on the road.

Jo's last duty in the show was to stand on the head of Maggie, the key elephant in the finale's long mount. Sturdy and dependable, Maggie stood firm while four elephants on each side of her rose on their hind legs, resting their front legs on the back of the one in front. Atop Maggie's broad head, Jo stood glittering under the lights with both arms lifted in the air. It was here, more than any other part of the show, that the applause washed over her. It merged with the music, the ringmaster's whistle, the laughter of children. Where she had been weary, she was now filled with energy. She knew the fatigue would return, so she relished the power of the moment all the more. For those few seconds there was no work, no long hours, no predawn drives. There was only magic. Even when it was over and she slid from Maggie's back, she could still feel it.

Outside the tent, troupers and roustabouts and shandies mingled. There were anecdotes to exchange, performances to dissect, observations to be made. Gradually, they drifted away alone, in pairs or in groups. Some would change and help strike the tents, some would sleep, some would worry over their performances. Too energized to sleep, Jo planned to assist in the striking of the Big Top.

She switched on a low light as she entered her trailer, then absently braided her hair as she moved to the tiny bath. With quick moves she creamed off her stage makeup. The exotic exaggeration of her eyes was whisked away, leaving the thick fringe of her lashes and the dark green of her irises unenhanced. The soft bloom of natural rose tinted her cheeks again, and her mouth, unpainted, appeared oddly vulnerable. Accustomed to the change, Jo did not see the sharp contrast between Jovilette the performer and the small, somewhat fragile woman in the glittering jumpsuit. With her face naked and the simple braid hanging down her back, the look of the wild, of the gypsy, was less apparent. It remained in her movements, but her face rinsed of all artifice and unframed, was both delicate and young, part ingenue, part flare. But Jo saw none of this as she reached for her front zipper. Before she could pull it down, a knock sounded on her door.

"Come in," she called out and flicked her braid behind her back as she started down the aisle. She stopped in her tracks as Keane stepped through the door.

"Didn't anyone ever tell you to ask who it is first?" He shut the door behind him and locked it with a careless flick of his wrist. "You might not have to lock your door against the circus people," he continued blandly as she remained still, "but there are several dozen curious towners still hanging around."

"I can handle a curious towner," Jo replied. The offhand quality of his dominance was infuriating. "I never lock my door."

There was stiffness and annoyance in her voice. Keane ignored them both. "I brought you something from Chicago."

The casual statement succeeded in throwing Jo's temper off the mark. For the first time, she noticed the small package he carried. "What is it?" she asked.

Keane smiled and crossed to her. "It's nothing that bites," he assured her, then held it out.

Still cautious, Jo lifted her eyes to his, then dropped her gaze back to the package. "It's not my birthday," she murmured.

"It's not Christmas, either," Keane pointed out.

The easy patience in the tone caused Jo to lift her eyes again. She wondered how it was he understood her hesitation to accept presents. She kept her gazed locked on his. "Thank you," she said solemnly as she took the gift.

"You're welcome," Keane returned in the same tone.

The amenities done, Jo recklessly ripped the paper. "Oh! It's Dante," she exclaimed, tearing off the remaining paper and tossing it on the table. With reverence she ran her palm over the dark leather binding. The rich scent drifted to her. She knew her quota of books would have been limited to one a year had she bought a volume so handsomely bound. She opened it slowly, as if to prolong the pleasure. The pages were heavy and rich cream in color. The text was Italian, and even as she glanced over the first page, the words ran fluidly through her mind.

"It's beautiful," she murmured, overcome. Lifting her eyes to thank him again, Jo found Keane smiling down at her. Shyness enveloped her suddenly, all the more intense because she had so rarely experienced it. A lifetime in front of crowds had given her a natural confidence in almost any situation. Now color began to surge into her cheeks, and her mind was a jumble of words that would not come to order.

"I'm glad you like it." He ran a finger down her cheek. "Do you always blush when someone gives you a present?"

Because she was at a loss as to how to answer his question, Jo maneuvered around it. "It was nice of you to think of me."

"It seems to come naturally," Keane replied, then watched Jo's lashes flutter down.

"I don't know what to say." She was able to meet his eyes again with her usual directness, but he had again touched her emotions. She felt inadequate to deal with her feelings or with his effect on her.

"You've already said it." He took the book from Jo's hand and paged through it. "Of course, I can't read a word of it. I envy you that." Before Jo could ponder the idea of a man like Keane Prescott envying her anything, he looked back up and smiled. Her thoughts scattered like nervous ants. "Got any coffee?" he asked and set the book back down on the table.

"Coffee?"

"Yes, you know, coffee. They grow it in quantity in Brazil."

Jo gave him a despairing look. "I don't have any made. I'd fix you a cup, but I've got to change before I help strike the tents. The cookhouse will still be serving."

Keane lifted a brow as he let his eyes wander over her face. "Don't you think that between Bo Peep, lions and butterflies, you've done enough work tonight? By the way, you make a very appealing butterfly."

"Thank you, but——"

"Let's put it this way," Keane countered smoothly. He took the tip of her braid in his fingers. "You've got the night off. I'll make the coffee myself if you show me where you keep it."

Though she let out a windy sigh, Jo was more amused than annoyed. Coffee, she decided, was the least she could do after he had brought her such a lovely present. "I'll make it," she told him, "but you'll probably wish you'd gone to the cookhouse." With this dubious invitation, Jo turned and headed toward the kitchen. He made no sound, but she knew he followed her. For the first time, she felt the smallness of her kitchen.

Setting an undersized copper kettle on one of the two burners, Jo flicked on the power. It was a simple matter to keep her back to him while she plucked cups from the cupboard. She was well aware that if she turned around in the compact kitchen, she would all but be in his arms.

"Did you watch the whole show?" she asked conversationally as she pulled out a jar of instant coffee.

"Duffy had me working props," Keane answered. "He seems to be making me generally useful."

Amused, Jo twisted her head to grin at him. Instantly, she discovered her misstep in strategy. Keane's face was only inches from hers, and in his eyes she read his thoughts. He wanted her, and he intended to have her. Before she could shift her position, Keane took her shoulders and turned her completely around. Jo knew she had backed up against the bars.

Leisurely, he began to loosen her hair, working his fingers through it until it pooled over her shoulders. "I've wanted to do that since the first time I saw you. It's hair to get lost in." His voice was soft as he took a generous handful. The gesture itself seemed to stake his claim. "In the sun it shimmers with red lights, but in the dark it's like night itself." It came to her that each time she was close to him, she was less able to resist him. She became more lost in his eyes, more beguiled by his power. Already her mouth tingled with the memory of his kiss, with the longing for a new one. Behind them the kettle began a feverish whistle.

"The water," she managed and tried to move around him. With one hand in her hair, Keane kept her still as he turned off the burner. The whistle sputtered peevishly, then died. The sound echoed in Jo's head.

"Do you want coffee?" he murmured as his fingers trailed to her throat.

Jo's eyes clung to his. Hers were enormous and direct, his quiet and searching. "No," she whispered, knowing she wanted nothing more at that moment than to belong to him. He circled her throat with his hand and pressed his fingers against her pulse. It fluttered wildly.

"You're trembling." He could feel the light tremor of her body as he brought her closer. "Is it fear?" he demanded as his thumbs brushed over her lips. "Or excitement?"

"Both," she answered in a voice thickened with emotion. She made a tiny, confused sound as his palm covered her heart. Its desperate thudding increased. "Are you..." She stopped a moment because her voice was breathless and unsteady. "Are you going to make love to me?" Did his eyes really darken? she wondered dizzily. Or is it my imagination?

"Beautiful Jovilette," he murmured as his mouth lowered to hers. "No pretentions, no evasions...irresistible." The quality of the kiss altered swiftly. His mouth was hungry on hers, and her response leaped past all caution. If loving him was madness, her heart reasoned, could making love take her further beyond sanity? Past wisdom and steeped in sensation, she let her heart rule her will. When her lips parted under his, it was not in surrender but in equal demand.

Keane gentled the kiss. He kept her shimmering on the razor's edge of passion. His mouth teased, promised, then fed her growing need. He found the zipper at the base of her throat and pulled it downward slowly. Her skin was warm, and he sought it, giving a low sound of pleasure as her breast swelled under his hand. He explored without hurry, as if memorizing each curve and plane. Jo no longer trembled but became pliant as her body moved to the rhythm he set. Her sigh was spontaneous, filled with wonder and delight.

With a suddenness that took her breath away, Keane crushed her mouth beneath his in fiery urgency. Jo's instincts responded, thrusting her into a world she had only imagined. His hands grew rougher, more insistent. Jo realized he had relinquished control. They were both riding on the tossing waves of passion. This sea had no horizon and no depth. It was a drowning sea that pulled the unsuspecting under while promising limitless pleasure. Jo did not resist but dove deeper.

At first she thought the knocking was only the sound of her heart against her ribs. When Keane drew away, she murmured in protest and pulled him back. Instantly, his mouth was avid, but as the knocking continued, he swore and pulled back again.

"Someone's persistent," he muttered. Bewildered, Jo stared up at him. "The door," he explained on a long breath.

"Oh." Flustered, Jo ran a hand through her hair and tried to collect her wits.

"You'd better answer it," Keane suggested as he pulled the zipper to her throat in one quick move. Jo broke the surface into reality abruptly. For a moment Keane watched her, taking in her flushed cheeks and tousled hair before he moved aside. Willing her legs to carry her, Jo walked to the front of the trailer. The door handle resisted, then she remembered that Keane had locked it, and she turned the latch.

"Yes, Buck?" she said calmly enough when she opened the door to her handler.

"Jo." His face was in shadows, but she heard the distress in the single syllable. Her chest tightened. "It's Ari."

He had barely finished the name before Jo was out of the trailer and running across the compound. She found both Pete and Gerry standing near Ari's cage.

"How bad?" she demanded as Pete came to meet her.

He took her shoulders. "Really bad this time, Jo."

For a moment she wanted to shake her head, to deny what she read in Pete's eyes. Instead, she nudged him aside and walked to Ari's cage. The old cat lay on his side as his chest lifted and fell with the effort of breathing. "Open it," she ordered Pete in a voice that revealed nothing. There was the jingle of keys, but she did not turn.

"You're not going in there." Jo heard Keane's voice and felt a restraining grip on her shoulders. Her eyes were opaque as she looked up at him.

"Yes, I am. Ari isn't going to hurt me or anyone else. He's just going to die. Now leave me alone." Her voice was low and toneless. "Open it," she ordered again, then pulled out of Keane's loosened hold. The bars rattled as he slid the door open. Hearing it, Jo turned, then hoisted herself into the cage.

Ari barely stirred. Jo saw, as she knelt beside him, that his eyes were open. They were glazed with weariness and pain. "Ari," she sighed, seeing there would be no tomorrow for him. His only answer was a hollow wheezing. Putting a hand to his side, she felt the ragged pace of his breathing. He made an effort to respond to her touch, to his name, but managed only to shift his great head on the floor. The gesture tore at Jo's heart. She lowered her face to his mane, remembering him as he had once been: full of strength and a terrifying beauty. She lifted her face again and took one long, steadying breath. "Buck." She heard him approach but kept her eyes on Ari. "Get the medical kit. I want a hypo of pentobarbital." She could feel Buck's brief hesitation before he spoke.

"Okay, Jo."

She sat quietly, stroking Ari's head. In the distance were the sounds of the Big Top going down, the call of men, the rattle of rigging, the clang of wood against metal. An elephant trumpeted, and three cages down, Faust roared half-heartedly in response.

"Jo." She turned her head as Buck called her and pushed her hair from her eyes. "Let me do it."

Jo merely shook her head and held out her hand.

"Jo." Keane stepped up to the bars. His voice was gentle, but his eyes were so like the cat's at her knees, Jo nearly sobbed aloud. "You don't have to do this yourself."

"He's my cat," she responded dully. "I said I'd do it when it was time. It's time." Her eyes shifted to Buck. "Give me the hypo, Buck. Let's get it done." When the syringe was in her hand, Jo stared at it, then closed her fingers around it. Swallowing hard, she turned back to Ari. His eyes were on her face. After more than twenty years in captivity there was still something not quite tamed in the dying cat. But she saw trust in his eyes and wanted to weep. "You were the best," she told him as she passed a hand through his mane. "You were always the best." Jo felt a numbing cold settling over her and prayed it would last until she had finished. "You're tired now. I'm going to help you sleep." She pulled the safety from the point of the hypodermic and waited until she was certain her hands were steady. "This won't hurt, nothing is going to hurt you anymore."

Involuntarily, Jo rubbed the back of her hand over her mouth, then, moving quickly, she plunged the needle into Ari's shoulder. A quiet whimper escaped her as she emptied the syringe. Ari made no sound but continued to watch her face. Jo offered no words of comfort but sat with him, methodically stroking his fur as his eyes grew cloudy. Gradually, the effort of his breathing lessened, becoming quieter and quieter until it wasn't there at all. Jo felt him grow still, and her hand balled into a fist inside the mass of his mane. One quick, convulsive shudder escaped her. Steeling herself, she moved from the cage, closing the door behind her. Because her bones felt fragile, she kept them stiff, as though they might shatter. Even as she stepped back to the ground, Keane took her arm and began to lead her away.

"Take care of things," he said to Buck as they moved past.

"No." Jo protested, trying and failing to free her arm. "I'll do it."

"No, you won't." Keane's tone held a quiet finality. "Enough's enough."

"Don't tell me what to do," she said sharply, letting her grief take refuge in anger.

"I *am* telling you," he pointed out. His hand was firm on her arm.

"You *can't* tell me what to do," she insisted as tears rose treacherously in her throat. "I want you to leave me alone."

Keane stopped, then took her by the shoulders. His eyes caught the light of a waning moon. "There's no way I'm going to leave you alone when you're so upset."

"My emotions have nothing to do with you." Even as she spoke, he took her arm again and pulled her toward her trailer. Jo wanted desperately to be alone to weep out her grief in private. The mourning belonged to her, and the tears were personal. As if her protests were nonexistent, he pulled her into the trailer and closed the door behind them. "Will you get out of here?" she demanded, frantically swallowing tears.

"Not until I know you're all right." Keane's answer was calm as he walked back to the kitchen.

"I'm perfectly all right." Her breath shuddered in and out quickly. "Or I will be when you leave me alone. You have no right to poke your nose in my business."

"So you've told me before," Keane answered mildly from the back of the trailer.

"I just did what had to be done." She held her body rigid and fought against her own quick, uneven breathing. "I put a sick animal out of his misery; it's as simple as that." Her voice broke, and she turned away, hugging her arms. "For heaven's sake, Keane, go away!"

Quietly, he walked back to her carrying a glass of water. "Drink this."

"No." She whirled back to him. Tears spilled out of her eyes and trickled down her cheeks despite her efforts to banish them. Hating herself, she pressed the heel of her hand between her brows and closed her eyes. "I don't want you here." Keane set down the glass, then gathered her into his arms. "No, don't. I don't want you to hold me."

"Too bad." He ran a hand gently up and down her back. "You did a very brave thing, Jo. I know you loved Ari. I know how hard it was to let him go. You're hurting, and I'm not leaving you."

"I don't want to cry in front of you." Her fists were tight balls at his shoulders.

"Why not?" The stroking continued up and down her back as he cradled her head in the curve of his shoulder.

"Why won't you let me be?" she sobbed as her control slipped. Her fingers gripped his shirt convulsively. "Why am I always losing what I love?" She let the grief come. She let his arms soothe her. As desperately as she had protested against it, she clung to his offer of comfort.

She made no objection as he carried her to the couch and cradled her in his arms. He stroked her hair, as she had stroked Ari, to ease the pain of what couldn't be changed. Slowly, her sobbing quieted. Still she lay with her cheek against his chest, with her hair curtaining her face.

"Better?" he asked as the silence grew calmer. Jo nodded, not yet trusting her voice. Keane shifted her as he reached for the glass of water. "Drink this now."

Gratefully, Jo relieved her dry throat, then went without resistance back against his chest. She closed her eyes, thinking it had been a very long time since she had been held in anyone's lap and soothed. "Keane," she murmured. She felt his lips brush over the top of her head.

"Hmm?"

"Nothing." Her voice thickened as she drifted toward sleep. "Just Keane."

Chapter Eight

Jo felt the sun on her closed lids. There was the summer morning sound of excited birds. Her mind, levitating slowly toward the surface, told her it must be Monday. Only on Monday would she sleep past sunrise. That was the enroute day, the only day in seven the circus held no show. She thought lazily of getting up. She would set aside two hours for reading. Maybe I'll drive into town and see a movie. What town are we in? With a sleepy sigh she rolled onto her stomach.

I'll give the cats a good going over, maybe hose them down if it gets hot enough. Memory flooded back and snapped her awake. *Ari.* Opening her eyes, Jo rolled onto her back and stared at the ceiling. Now she recalled vividly how the old cat had died with his eyes trusting on her face. She sighed again. The sadness was still there, but not the sharp, desperate grief of the night before. Acceptance was settling in. She realized that Keane's insistence on staying with her during the peak of her mourning had helped her. He had given her someone to rail at, then someone to hold on to. She remembered the incredible comfort of being cradled in his lap, the solid dependability of his chest against her cheek. She had fallen asleep with the sound of his heart in her ear.

Turning her head, Jo looked out the window, then at the patch of white light the sun tossed on the floor. But it isn't Monday, she remembered suddenly. It's Thursday. Jo sat up, pushing at her hair, which seemed to tumble everywhere at once. What was she doing in bed on a Thursday when the sun was up? Without giving herself time to work out the answer, she scrambled out of bed and hurried from the room. She gave a soft gasp as she ran headlong into Keane.

His hand ran down the length of her hair before he took her shoulder. "I heard you stirring," he said easily, looking down into her stunned face.

"What are you doing here?"

"Making coffee," he answered as he gave her a critical study. "Or I was a moment ago. How are you?"

"I'm all right." Jo lifted her hand to her temple as if to gain her bearings. "I'm a bit disoriented, I suppose. I overslept. It's never happened before."

"I gave you a sleeping pill," Keane told her matter-of-factly. He slipped an arm around her shoulder as he turned back to the kitchen.

"A pill?" Jo's eyes flew to his. "I don't remember taking a pill."

"It was in the water you drank." On the stove the kettle began its piercing whistle. Moving to it, Keane finished making the coffee. "I had my doubts as to whether you'd take it voluntarily."

"No, I wouldn't have," Jo agreed with some annoyance. "I've never taken a sleeping pill in my life."

"Well, you did last night." He held out a mug of coffee. "I sent Gerry for it while you were in the cage with Ari." Again he gave her a quick, intense study. "It didn't seem to do you any harm. You went out like a light. I carried you to bed, changed your clothes——"

"Changed my..." All at once Jo became aware that she wore only a thin white nightshirt. Her hand reached instinctively for the top button that nestled just above her bosom. Thinking hard, she found she could recall nothing beyond falling asleep in his arms.

"I don't think you'd have spent a very comfortable night in your costume," Keane pointed out. Enjoying his coffee, he smiled at the nervous hand she held between her breasts. "I've had a certain amount of experience undressing women in the dark." Jo dropped her hand. It was an unmistakable movement of pride. Keane's eyes softened. "You needed a good night's sleep, Jo. You were worn out."

Without speaking, Jo lifted her coffee to her lips and turned away. Walking to the window, she could see that the back yard was deserted. Her sleep must indeed have been deep to have kept her unaware of camp breaking.

"Everyone's gone but a couple of roustabouts and a generator truck. They'll take off when you don't need power anymore."

The vulnerability Jo felt was overwhelming. Several times in the course of the evening before, she had lost control, which had always been an essential part of her. Each time, it had been Keane who had been there. She wanted to be angry with him for intruding on her privacy but found it impossible. She had needed him, and he had known it.

"You didn't have to stay behind," she said, watching a crow swoop low over the ground outside.

"I wasn't certain you'd be in any shape to drive fifty miles this morning. Pete's driving my trailer."

Her shoulders lifted and fell before she turned around. Sunlight streamed through the window at her back and poured through the thin folds of her nightshirt. Her body was a slender shadow. When she spoke, her voice was low with regret. "I was horribly rude to you last night."

Keane shrugged and lifted his coffee. "You were upset."

"Yes." Her eyes were an open reflection of her sorrow. "Ari was very important to me. I suppose he was an ongoing link with my father, with my childhood. I'd known for some time he wouldn't make it through the season, but I didn't want to face it.'' She looked down at the mug she held gripped in both hands. A faint wisp of steam rose from it and vanished. ''Last night was a relief for him. It was selfish of me to wish it otherwise. And I was wrong to strike out at you the way I did. I'm sorry.''

''I don't want your apology, Jo.'' Because he sounded annoyed, she looked up quickly.

''I'd feel better if you'd take it, Keane. You've been very kind.''

To her astonishment, he swore under his breath and turned back to the stove. ''I don't care for your gratitude any more than your apology.'' He set down his mug and poured in more coffee. ''Neither of them is necessary.''

''They are to me,'' Jo replied, then took a step toward him. ''Keane . . .'' She set down her coffee and touched his arm. When he turned, she let impulse guide her. She rested her head on his shoulder and slipped her arms around his waist. He stiffened, putting his hands to her shoulders as if to draw her away. Then she heard his breath come out in a long sigh as he relaxed. For an instant he brought her closer.

''I never know precisely what to expect from you,'' he murmured. He lifted her chin with his finger. In automatic response, Jo closed her eyes and offered her mouth. She felt his fingers tighten on her skin before his lips brushed hers lightly. ''You'd better go change.'' His manner was friendly but cool as he stepped away. "We'll stop off in town, and I'll buy you some breakfast."

Puzzled by his attitude but satisfied he was no longer annoyed, Jo nodded. "All right."

Spring became summer as the circus wound its way north. The sun stayed longer, peeking into the Big Top until well after the evening show began. Heavy rain came infrequently, but there were quick summer storms with thunder and lightning. Through June, Prescott's Circus Colossus snaked through North Carolina and into western Tennessee.

During the long weeks while spring tripped over into summer, Jo found Keane's attitude a paradox. His friendliness toward her was offhand. He laughed if she said something amusing, listened if she had a complaint and to her confusion, slipped a thin barrier between them. At times she wondered if the passion that had flared between them the night he had returned from Chicago had truly existed. Had the desire she had tasted on his lips been a fantasy? The closeness she had felt blooming between them had withered and blown away. They were only owner and trouper now.

Keane flew back to Chicago twice more during this period, but he brought no surprise presents back with him. Not once during those long weeks did he come by her trailer. Initially, his al-

tered manner confused her. He was not angry.
His mood was neither heated nor icy with temper but fell into an odd middle ground she could
not understand. Jo ached with love. As days
passed into weeks, she was forced to admit that
Keane did not seem to be interested in a close relationship.

On the eve of the July Fourth show, Jo sat
sleepless in her bed. In her hand she held the volume of Dante, but the book was only a reminder
of the emptiness she felt. She closed it, then
stared at the ceiling. It's time to snap out of it,
she lectured herself. It's time to stop pretending
he was ever really part of my life. Loving someone only makes him a part of your wishes. He
never talked about love, he never promised anything, never offered anything but what he gave to
me. He's done nothing to hurt me. Jo squeezed
her eyes shut and pressed the book between her
fingers. How I wish I could hate him for showing me what life could be like and then turning
away, she thought.

But I can't. Jo let out a shaky breath and relaxed her grip on the book. Gently, she ran a finger down its smooth, leather binding. I can't hate
him, but I can't love him openly, either. How do
I stop? I should be grateful he stopped wanting
me. I would have made love with him. Then I'd
hurt a hundred times more. Could I hurt a hun-

dred times more? For several moments she lay still, trying to quiet her thoughts.

It's best not to know, she told herself sternly. It's best to remember he was kind to me when I needed him and that I haven't a right to make demands. Summer doesn't last forever. I may never see him again when it's over. At least I can keep the time we have pleasant.

The words sounded hollow in her heart.

Chapter Nine

The Fourth of July was a full day with a run to a new lot, the tent raising, a street parade and two shows. But it was a holiday. Elephants wore red, white and blue plumes atop their massive heads. The evening performance would be held an hour earlier to allow for the addition of a fireworks display. Traditionally, Prescott's circus arranged to spend the holiday in the same small town in Tennessee. The license and paperwork for the display were seen to in advance, and the fireworks were shipped ahead to be stored in a warehouse. The procedure had been precisely the same for years. It was one of the circus's most profitable nights. Concessions thrived.

Jo moved through the day with determined cheerfulness. She refused to permit the distance between her and Keane to spoil one of the highlights of the summer. Brooding, she decided, would not change things. The mood of the crowd helped to keep her spirits light.

Between shows came the inevitable lull. Some troupers sat outside their trailers exchanging small talk and enjoying the sun. Others got in a bit more practice or worked out a few kinks. Bull hands washed down the elephants, causing a minor flood in the pen area.

Jo watched the bathing process with amusement. She never ceased to enjoy this particular aspect of circus life, especially if there were one or two inexperienced bull hands involved. Invariably, Maggie or one of the other veteran bulls would spray a trunkful of water over the new hands to initiate them. Though Jo knew the other hands encouraged it, they always displayed remarkable innocence.

Spotting Duffy, Jo moved away from the elephant area and wandered toward him. She could see he was deep in discussion with a towner. He was as short as Duffy but wider, with what she had once heard Frank call a successful frame. His stomach started high and barreled out to below his waist. He had a ruddy complexion and pale eyes that squinted hard against the sun. Jo had seen his type before. She wondered what he was selling and how much he wanted for it. Since Duffy was puffing with annoyance, Jo assumed it was quite a lot.

"I'm telling you, Carlson, we've already paid for storage. I've got a signed receipt. And we pay fifteen bucks delivery, not twenty."

Carlson was smoking a small, unfiltered cigarette and dropped it to the ground. "You paid Myers for storage, not me. I bought the place six weeks ago." He shrugged his wide shoulders. "Not my problem you paid in advance."

Looking over, Jo saw Keane approaching with Pete. Pete was talking rapidly, Keane nodding. As Jo watched, Keane glanced up and gave Carlson a quick study. She had seen that look before and knew the older man had been assessed. Keane caught her eye, smiled and began to move past her. "Hello, Jo."

Unashamedly curious, Jo fell into step beside him. "What's going on?"

"Why don't we find out?" he suggested as they stopped in front of Duffy and Carlson. "Gentlemen," Keane said in an easy tone. "Is there a problem?"

"This character," Duffy spouted, jerking a scornful thumb at Carlson's face, "wants us to pay twice for storage on the fireworks. Then he wants twenty for delivery when we agreed on fifteen."

"Myers agreed on fifteen," Carlson pointed out. He smiled without humor. "I didn't agree on anything. You want your fireworks, you gotta pay for them first—cash," he added, then spared Keane a glance. "Who's this guy?"

Duffy began to wheeze with indignation, but Keane laid a restraining hand on his shoulder. "I'm Prescott," he told him in untroubled tones. "Perhaps you'd like to fill me in."

"Prescott, huh?" Carlson stroked both his chins as he studied Keane. Seeing youth and amiable eyes, he felt closer to success. "Well, now we're getting somewhere," he said jovially and stuck out his hand. Keane accepted it without hesitation. "Jim Carlson," he continued as he gave Keane's hand a brisk pump. "Nice circus you got here, Prescott. Me and the missus see it every year. Well, now," he said again and hitched up his belt. "Seeing as you're a businessman, too, I'm sure we can straighten all this out. Problem is, your fireworks've been stored in my warehouse. Now, I gotta make a living, they can't just sit there for free. I bought the place off Myers six weeks ago. I can't be held responsible for a deal you made with him, can I?" Carlson gave a stretched-lip smile, pleased that Keane listened so politely. "And as for delivery, well . . ." He made a helpless gesture and patted Keane's shoulder. "You know about gas prices these days, son. But we can work that out after we settle this other little problem."

Keane nodded agreeably. "That sounds reasonable." He ignored Duffy's huffing and puffing. "You do seem to have a problem, Mr. Carlson."

"I don't have a problem," Carlson countered. His smile suffered a fractional slip. "You've got the problem, unless you don't want the fireworks."

"Oh, we'll have the fireworks, Mr. Carlson," Keane corrected with a smile Jo thought more wolfish than friendly. "According to paragraph three, section five, of the small business code, the lessor is legally bound by all contracts, agreements, liens and mortgages of the previous lessor until such time as all aforesaid contracts, agreements, liens and mortgages are expired or transferred.''

''What the...'' Carlson began with no smile at all, but Keane continued blandly.

''Of course, we won't pursue the matter in court as long as we get our merchandise. But that doesn't solve your problem.''

''My problem?'' Carlson sputtered while Jo looked on in frank admiration. ''I haven't got a problem. If you think...''

''Oh, but you do, Mr. Carlson, though I'm sure there was no intent to break the law on your part.''

''Break the law?'' Carlson wiped damp hands on his slacks.

''Storing explosives without a license,'' Keane pointed out. ''Unless, of course, you obtained one after your purchase of the warehouse.''

''Well, no, I...''

''I was afraid of that.'' Keane lifted his brow in pity. ''You see, in paragraph six of section five of the small business code it states that all licenses, permits and warrants shall be nontransferable. Authorization for new licenses, permits or warrants must be requested in writing by the current owner. Notarized, naturally.'' Keane waited a bit to allow Carlson to wrestle with the idea. ''If I'm not mistaken,'' he continued conversationally, "the fine's pretty hefty in this state. Of course, sentencing depends on——"

"Sentencing?" Carlson paled and mopped the back of his neck with a handkerchief.

"Look, tell you what." Keane gave Carlson a sympathetic smile. "You get the fireworks over here and off your property. We don't have to bring the law in on something like this. Just an oversight, after all. We're both businessmen, aren't we?"

Too overwrought to detect sarcasm, Carlson nodded.

"That was fifteen on delivery, right?"

Carlson didn't hesitate but stuck the damp handkerchief back in his pocket and nodded again.

"Good enough. I'll have the cash for you on delivery. Glad to help you out."

Relieved, Carlson turned and headed for his pickup. Jo managed to keep her features grave until he pulled off the lot. Simultaneously, Pete and Duffy began to hoot with laughter.

"Was it true?" Jo demanded and took Keane's arm.

"Was what true?" Keane countered, merely lifting a brow over the hysterics that surrounded him.

"'Paragraph three, section five, of the small business code,'" Jo quoted.

"Never heard of it," Keane answered mildly, nearly sending Pete into orbit.

"You made it up," Jo said in wonder. "You made it all up!"

"Probably," Keane agreed.

"Smoothest con job I've seen in years," Duffy stated and gave Keane a parental slap on the back. "Son, you could go into business."

"I did," Keane told him and grinned.

"I ever need a lawyer," Pete put in, pushing his cap further back on his head, "I know where to go. You come on by the cookhouse tonight, Captain. We're having ourselves a poker game. Come on, Duffy, Buck's gotta hear about this."

As they moved off, Jo realized that Keane had been officially accepted. Before, he had been the legal owner but an outsider, a towner. Now he was one of them. Turning, she lifted her face to his. "Welcome aboard."

"Thank you." She saw he understood precisely what had been left unsaid.

"I'll see you at the game," she said before her smile became a grin. "Don't forget your money."

She turned away, but Keane touched her arm, bringing her back to him. "Jo," he began, puzzling her by the sudden seriousness of his eyes.

"Yes?"

There was a brief hesitation, then he shook his head. "Nothing, never mind. I'll see you later." He rubbed his knuckles over her cheek, then walked away.

* * *

Jo studied her hand impassively. On the deal, she had missed a heart flush by one card and now waited for someone to open. Casually, she moved her glance around the table. Duffy was puffing on a cigar, apparently unconcerned with the dwindling chips in front of him. Pete chewed his gum with equal nonchalance. Amy, the wife of the sword swallower, sat beside him, then Jamie, then Raoul. Directly beside Jo was Keane, who, like Pete, was winning consistently.

The pot grew. Chips clinked on the table. Jo discarded and was pleased to exchange a club for the fifth heart. She slipped it into her hand without blinking. Frank had taught her the game. Before the second round of betting Jamie folded in disgust. "Should never have taken Buck's seat," he muttered and frowned when Pete raised the bet.

"You got out cheap, kiddo," Duffy told him dolefully as he tossed in chips. "I'm only staying in so I don't change my standard of living. Money'll do that to you," he mumbled obscurely.

"Three kings," Pete announced when called, then spread his cards. Amid a flutter of complaints cards were tossed down.

"Heart flush," Jo said mildly before Pete could rake in the pot. Duffy leaned back and gave a hoot of laughter.

"Atta, girl, Jo. I hate to see him win all my money."

During the next two hours the cookhouse tent grew hot and ripe with the scents of coffee and tobacco and beer. Jamie's luck proved so consistently poor that he called for Buck to relieve him.

Jo found herself with an indifferent pair of fives. Almost immediately the betting grew heavy as Keane raised Raoul's opening. Curiosity kept Jo in one round, but practicality had her folding after the draw. Divorced from the game, she watched it with interest. Leaning on her elbows, she studied each participant. Keane played a good game, she mused. His eyes gave nothing away. They never did. Casually, he nursed the beer beside him while Duffy, Buck and Amy folded. Studying him closely, Pete chewed his gum. Keane returned the look, keeping the stub of his cigar clamped between his teeth. Raoul muttered in French and scowled at his cards.

"Could be bluffing," Pete considered, seeing Keane's raise. "Let's raise it five more and see what's cooking." Raoul swore in French, then again in English, before he tossed in his hand. Taking his time, Keane counted out the necessary chips and tossed them into the pot. It was a plastic mountain of red, white and blue. Then, he counted out more.

"I'll see your five," he said evenly, "and raise it ten."

There was mumbling around the table. Pete looked into his hand and considered. Shifting his eyes, he took in the generous pile of chips in front of him. He could afford to risk another ten. Glancing up, he studied Keane's face while he fondled his chips. Abruptly, he broke into a grin.

"Nope," he said simply, turning his cards face down. "This one's all yours."

Setting down his cards, Keane raked in a very sweet pot. "Gonna show 'em?" Pete asked. His grin was affable.

Keane pushed a stray chip into the pile and shrugged. With his free hand he turned over the cards. The reaction ranged from oaths to laughter.

"Trash," Pete mumbled with a shake of his head. "Nothing but trash. You've got nerve, Captain." His grin grew wide as he turned over his own cards. "Even I had a pair of sevens."

Raoul gnashed his teeth and swore elegantly in two languages. Jo grinned at his imaginative choice of words. She rose on a laugh and snatched off the soft felt hat Jamie wore. Deftly, she scooped her chips into it. "Cash me in later," she requested, then gave him a smacking kiss on the mouth. "But don't play with them."

Duffy scowled over at her. "Aren't you cashing in early?"

"You've always told me to leave 'em wanting more," she reminded him. With a grin and a wave, she swung through the door.

"That Jo," said Raoul, chuckling as he shuffled the cards. "She's one smart cracker."

"Cookie," Pete corrected, opening a fresh stick of gum. He noticed that Keane's gaze had drifted to the door she had closed behind her. "Some looker, too," he commented and watched Keane's eyes wander back to his. "Don't you think, Captain?"

Keane slipped his cards into a pile as they were dealt to him. "Jo's lovely."

"Like her mother," Buck put in, frowning at his cards. "She was a beaut, huh, Duffy?" Duffy grunted in agreement and wondered why Lady Luck refused to smile on him. "Always thought it was a crime for her to die that way. Wilder, too," he added with a shake of his head.

"A fire, wasn't it?" Keane asked as he picked up his cards and spread them.

"Electrical fire." Buck nodded and lifted his beer. "A short in their trailer's wiring. What a waste. If they hadn't been in bed asleep, they'd probably still be alive. The trailer was halfway gone before anybody set up an alarm. Just plain couldn't get to the Wilders. Their side of the trailer was like a furnace. Jo's bedroom was on the other side, and we nearly lost her. Frank busted in the window and pulled her out. Poor little tyke. She was holding onto this old doll like it was the last thing she had left. Kept it with her for I don't know how long. Remember, Duffy?" He glanced into his hand and opened for two. "It only had one arm." Duffy grunted again and folded. "Frank sure knew how to handle that little girl."

"She knew how to handle him, more likely," Duffy mumbled. Raoul bumped the pot five, and Keane folded.

"Deal me out the next hand," he said as he rose and moved to the door. One of the Gribalti brothers took the chair Jo had vacated, and Jamie slipped into Keane's. Curious, he lifted the tip of the cards. He saw a jack-high straight. With a thoughtful frown, he watched the door swing shut.

Outside, Jo moved through the warm night. With a glance at the sky, she thought of the fireworks. They had been wonderful, she mused, stirring up the stars with exploding color. Though it was over and a new day hovered, she felt some magic remained in the night. Far from sleepy, she wandered toward the Big Top.

"Hello, pretty lady."

Jo looked into the shadows and narrowed her eyes. She could just barely make out a form. "Oh, you're Bob, aren't you?" She stopped and gave him a friendly smile. "You're new."

He stepped toward her. "I've been on for nearly three weeks." He was young, Jo guessed about her own age, with a solid build and sharp-featured face. Just that afternoon she had watched Maggie give him a shower.

Jo pushed her hands into the pockets of her cut-offs and continued to smile. It appeared he thought his tenure made him a veteran. "How do you like working with the elephants?"

"It's okay. I like putting up the tent."

Jo understood his feeling. "So do I. There's a game in the cookhouse," she told him with a gesture of her arm. "You might like to sit in."

"I'd rather be with you." As he moved closer, Jo caught the faint whiff of beer. He's been celebrating, she thought and shook her head.

"It's a good thing tomorrow's Monday," she commented. "No one's going to be in any shape to pitch a tent. You should go to bed," she suggested. "Or get some coffee."

"Let's go to your trailer." Bob weaved a little, then took her arm.

"No." Firmly, Jo turned in the opposite direction. "Let's go to the cookhouse." His advances did not trouble her. She was close enough to the cookhouse tent that if she called out, a dozen able-bodied men would come charging. But that was precisely what Jo wanted to avoid.

"I want to go with you," he said, stumbling over the words as he veered away from the cookhouse again. "You look so pretty in that cage with those lions." He put both arms around her, but Jo felt it was as much for balance as romance. "A fella needs a pretty lady once in a while."

"I'm going to feed you to my lions if you don't let me go," Jo warned.

"Bet you can be a real wildcat," he mumbled and made a fumbling dive for her mouth.

Though her patience was wearing thin, Jo endured the kiss that landed slightly to the left of bull's-eye. His hands, however, had better aim and grabbed the firm roundness of her bottom. Losing her temper, Jo pushed away but found his hold had taken root. In a quick move, she brought up her fist and caught him square on the jaw. With only a faint sound of surprise, Bob sat down hard on the ground.

"Well, so much for rescuing you," Keane commented from behind her.

Turning quickly, Jo pushed at her hair and gave an annoyed sigh. She would have preferred no witnesses. Even in the dim light, she could see he was furious. Instinctively, she stepped between him and the man who sat on the ground fingering his jaw and shaking the buzzing from his ears.

"He—Bob just got a bit overenthusiastic," she said hastily and put a restraining hand on Keane's arm. "He's been celebrating."

"I'm feeling a bit enthusiastic myself," Keane stated. As he made to brush her aside, Jo clung with more fervor.

"No, Keane, please."

Looking down, he fired a glare. "Jo, would you let go so that I can deal with this?"

"Not until you listen." The faint hint of laughter in her eyes only enraged him further, and Jo fought to suppress it. "Keane, please, don't be hard on him. He didn't hurt me."

"He was attacking you," Keane interrupted. He barely resisted the urge to shake her off and drag the still seated Bob by the scruff of the neck.

"No, he was really more just leaning on me. His balance is a trifle impaired. He only tried to kiss me," she pointed out, wisely deleting the wandering hands. "And I hit him much harder than I should have. He's new, Keane, don't fire him."

Exasperated, he stared at her. "Firing was the least of what I had in mind for him."

Jo smiled, unable to keep the gleam from her eyes. "If you were going to avenge my honor, he really didn't do much more than breathe on it. I don't think you should run him through for that. Maybe you could just put him in the stocks for a couple of days."

Keane swore under his breath, but a reluctant smile tugged at his mouth. Seeing it, Jo loosened her hold. "Miss Wilder wants to give you a break," he told the dazed Bob in a tough, no-nonsense voice that Jo decided he used for intimidating witnesses. "She has a softer heart than I do. Therefore, I won't knock you down several more times or kick you off the lot, as I had entertained doing." He paused, allowing Bob time to consider this possibility. "Instead, I'll let you sleep off your—enthusiasm." In one quick jerk, he pulled Bob to his feet. "But if I ever hear of you breathing uninvited on Miss Wilder or any other of my female employees, we'll go back to the first choice. And before I kick you out," he added with low menace, "I'll let it be known that you were decked by one punch from a hundred-pound woman."

"Yes, sir, Mr. Prescott," said Bob as clearly as possible.

"Go to bed," Jo said kindly, seeing him pale. "You'll feel better in the morning."

"Obviously," Keane commented as Bob lurched away, "you haven't done much drinking." He turned to Jo and grinned. "The one thing he's not going to feel in the morning is better." Jo smiled, pleased to have Keane talk to her without the thin shield of politeness. "And where," he asked and took her hand for examination, "did you learn that right jab?"

Jo laughed, allowing Keane's fingers to interlock with hers. "It would hardly have knocked him down if he hadn't already been tilting in that direction." Her face turned up to his and sparkled with starlight. In his eyes an expression she couldn't comprehend came and went. "Is something wrong?"

For a moment he said nothing. In her breast her heart began to hammer as she waited to be kissed. "No, nothing," he said. The moment was shattered. "Come on, I'll walk you back to your trailer."

"I wasn't going there." Wanting to put him back into an easy mood, she linked her arm with his. "If you come with me, I'll show you some magic." Her smile slanted invitingly. "You like magic, don't you, Keane? Even a sober, dedicated lawyer must like magic."

"Is that how I strike you?" Jo almost laughed at the trace of annoyance in his voice. "As a sober, dedicated lawyer?"

"Oh, not entirely, though that's part of you." She enjoyed feeling that for the moment she had him to herself. "You've also got a streak of adventure and a rather nice sense of humor. And," she added with generous emphasis, "there's your temper."

"You seem to have me all figured out."

"Oh, no." Jo stopped and turned to him. "Not at all. I only know how you are here. I can only speculate on how you are in Chicago."

His brow lifted as she caught his attention. "Would I be different there?"

"I don't know." Jo's forehead wrinkled in thought. "Wouldn't you be? Circumstances would. You probably have a house or a big apartment, and there's a housekeeper who comes in once—no, twice—a week." Caught up in the picture, she gazed off into the distance and built it further. "You have an office with a view of the city, a very efficient secretary and a brilliant law clerk. You go to business lunches at the club. In court you're deadly and very successful. You have your own tailor and work out at the gym three times a week. There's the theater on the weekends, along with something physical. Tennis maybe, not golf. No, handball.''

Keane shook his head. "Is this the magic?"

"No." Jo shrugged and began to walk again. "Just guesswork. You don't have to have a great deal of money to know how people who do behave. And I know you take the law seriously. You wouldn't choose a career that wasn't very important to you."

Keane walked in silence. When he spoke, his voice was quiet. "I'm not certain I'm comfortable with your little outline of my life."

"It's very sketchy," Jo told him. "I'd have to understand you better to fill in the gaps."

"Don't you?"

"What?" Jo asked, pausing. "Understand you?" She laughed, tickled at the absurdity of his question. "No, I don't understand you. How could I? You live in a different world." With this, she tossed aside the flap of the Big Top and stepped into its darkness. When she hit the switch, two rows of overhead lights flashed on. Shadows haunted the corners and fell over the arena seats.

"It's wonderful, isn't it?" Her clear voice ran the length of the tent and echoed back. "It's not empty, you know. They're always here—the troupers, the audience, the animals.'' She walked forward until she stood beside the third ring. ''Do you know what this is?'' she asked Keane, tossing out her arms and turning a full circle. ''It's an ageless wonder in a changing world. No matter what happens on the outside, this is here. We're the most fragile of circuses, at the mercy of the elephants, of emotions, of mechanics, of public whims. But six days a week for twenty-nine weeks we perform miracles. We build a world at dawn, then disappear into the dark. That's part of it— the mystery.'' She waited until Keane moved forward to join her.

''Tents pop up on an empty lot, elephants and lions walk down Main Street. And we never grow old, because each new generation discovers us all over again.'' She stood slender and exquisite in a circle of light. ''Life here's crazy. And it's hard. Muddy lots, insane hours, sore muscles, but when you've finished your act and you get that feeling that tells you it was special, there's nothing else like it in the world.''

''Is that why you do it?'' Keane asked.

Jo shook her head and moved out of the circle of light into the dark and into another ring. ''It's all part of the same thing. We all have our own reasons, I suppose. You've asked me that before; I'm not certain I can explain. Maybe it's that we all believe in miracles.'' She turned under the light, and it shimmered around her. ''I've been here all my life. I know every trick, every illusion. I know how Jamie's dad gets twenty clowns into a two-seater car. But each time I see it, I laugh and I believe it. It's not just the excitement, Keane, it's the anticipation of the excitement. It's knowing you're going to see the biggest or the smallest or the fastest or the highest." Jo ran to the center ring and threw up her arms.

"Ladies and gentlemen," she announced with a toss of her head. "For your amazement and astonishment, for the first time in America, a superabundance of mountainous, mighty pachyderms led in a stupendous exhibition of choreography by the Great Serena." Jo laughed and shifted her hair to her back with a quick movement of her hand. "Dancing elephants!" she said to Keane, pleased that he was smiling. "Or you listen to the talker in the sideshow when he starts his spiel. Step right up. Come a little closer." She curled her fingers in invitation. "See the Amazing Serpentina and her monstrous, slithering vipers. Watch the beautiful young girl charm a deadly cobra. Watch her accept the reptilian embrace of the gargantuan boa. Don't miss the chance to see the enchantress of the evil serpent!"

"I suppose Baby might sue for slander."

Jo laughed and stepped up on the ring. "But when the crowds see little Rose with a boa constrictor wrapped around her shoulders, they've gotten their money's worth. We give them what they come for: color, fantasy, the unique. Thrills.

You've seen the audience when Vito does his high wire act without a net."

"A net seems little enough protection when he's balancing on a wire at two hundred feet." Keane stuck his hands in his pockets and frowned. "He risks his life every day."

"So does a police officer or a fire fighter." Jo spoke quietly and rested her hands on his shoulders. It seemed more necessary than ever that she make him understand his father's dream. "I know what you're saying, Keane, but you have to understand us. The element of danger is essential to many of the acts. You can hear the whole audience suck in their breath when Vito does his back somersault on the wire. They'd be impressed if he used a net, but they wouldn't be terrified."

"Do they need to be?"

Jo's sober expression lightened. "Oh, yes! They need to be terrified and fascinated and mesmerized. It's all included in the price of a ticket. This is a world of superlatives. We test the limit of human daring, and every day it changes. Do you know how long it took before the first man accomplished the triple on the trapeze? Now it's nearly a standard." A light of anticipation flared in her eyes. "One day someone will do a quadruple. If a man stands in this ring and juggles three torches today, tomorrow someone will juggle them on horseback and after that there'll be a team tossing them back and forth while swinging on a trap. It's our job to do the incredible, then, when it's done, to do the impossible. It's that simple.''

"Simple," Keane murmured, then lifted a hand to caress her hair. "I wonder if you'd think so if you could see it from the outside.''

"I don't know." Her fingers tightened on his shoulders as he buried his other hand in her hair. "I never have.''

As if his thoughts centered on it, Keane combed his fingers through her hair. Gradually, he pushed it back until only his hands framed her face. They stood in a pool of light that threw their shadows long behind them. "You are so lovely," he murmured.

Jo neither spoke nor moved. There was something different this time in the way he touched her. There was a gentleness and a hesitation she had not felt before. Though they looked directly into hers, she could not read his eyes. Their faces were close, and his breath fluttered against her mouth. Jo slid her arms around his neck and pressed her mouth to his.

Not until that moment had she realized how empty she had felt, how desperately she had needed to hold him. Her lips were hungry for his. She clung while all gentleness fled from his touch. His hands were greedy. The weeks that he had not touched her were forgotten as her skin warmed and hummed with quickening blood. Passion stripped her of inhibitions, and her tongue sought

his, taking the kiss into wilder and darker depths.
Their lips parted, only to meet again with sharp
new demands. She understood that all needs and
all desires were ultimately only one—Keane.

His mouth left hers, and for an instant he
rested his cheek against her hair. For that moment Jo felt a contentment more complete than
she had ever known. Abruptly, he drew away.

Puzzled, she watched as he drew out a cigar.
She lifted a hand to run it through the hair he had
just disturbed. He flicked on his lighter.
"Keane?" She looked at him, knowing her eyes
offered everything.

"You've had a long day," he began in an oddly
polite tone. Jo winced as if he had struck her.
"I'll walk you back to your trailer."

She stepped off the ring and away from him.
Pain seared along her skin. "Why are you doing
this?" To her humiliation, tears welled in her eyes
and lodged in her throat. The tears acted as a
prism, refracting the light and clouding her vision. She blinked them back. Keane's brows drew
together at the gesture.

"I'll take you back," he said again. The detached tone of his voice accelerated all Jo's fury
and grief.

"How dare you!" she demanded. "How dare
you make me..." The word *love* nearly slipped
through her lips, and she swallowed it. "How
dare you make me want you, then turn away! I
was right about you from the beginning. I

thought I'd been wrong. You're cold and unfeeling." Her breath came quickly and unevenly, but she refused to retreat until she had said it all. Her face was pale with the passion of her emotions. "I don't know why I thought you'd ever understand what Frank had given you. You need a heart to see the intangible. I'll be glad when the season's over and you do whatever it is you're going to do. I'll be glad when I never have to see you again. I won't let you do this to me anymore!" Her voice wavered, but she made no attempt to steady it. "I don't want you to ever touch me again."

Keane studied her for a long moment, then took a careful drag on his cigar. "All right, Jo."

The very calmness of his answer tore a sob from her before she turned and ran from the Big Top.

Chapter Ten

In July the troupe circled through Virginia, touched the tip of West Virginia on their way into Kentucky, then moved into Ohio. Audiences fanned themselves as the temperatures in the Big Top rose, but they still came.

Since the evening of the Fourth, Jo had avoided Keane. It was not as difficult as it might have been, as he spent half the month in Chicago dealing with his business. Jo functioned. She ate because eating was necessary in order to maintain her strength. She slept because rest was essential to remaining alert in the cage. She did not find any enjoyment in food nor was her sleep restful. Because so many in the troupe knew her well, Jo struggled to keep on a mask of normalcy. Above all, she needed to avoid any questions, any advice, any sympathy. It was necessary, because of her profession, to put her emotions on hold a great deal of the time. After some struggle and some failure, Jo achieved a reasonable success.

Her training of Gerry continued, as did his progress. The additional duty of working with him helped fill her small snatches of spare time.

On afternoons when no matinee was scheduled,
Jo took him into the big cage. As he grew more
proficient, she brought other cats in to join Merlin. By the first week in August they were working together with her full complement of lions.

The only others who were rehearsing in the Big
Top were the equestrian act. They ran through
the Thread the Needle routine in the first ring.
Hooves echoed dully on tanbark. Jo supervised
while Gerry sent the cats into a pyramid. At his
urging, Lazarus climbed up the wide, arched
ladder that topped the grouping. Twice he
balked, and twice Gerry was forced to reissue the
command.

"Good," Jo commented when the pyramid
was complete.

"He wouldn't go." Gerry began to complain,
but she cut him off.

"Don't be in too much of a hurry. Bring them
down." Her tone was brisk and professional.
"Make certain they dismount and take their seats
in the right order. It's important to stick to routine."

Hands resting on hips, Jo watched. In her
opinion, Gerry had true potential. His nerves
were good, he had a feeling for the animals, and
he was slowly developing patience. Still she
balked at the next step in his training: leaving him
alone in the arena. Even with only Merlin, she
felt it too risky. He was still too casual. Not yet
did he possess enough respect for the lion's guile.

Jo moved around the arena, and the lions, used to her, were not disturbed. As the cats settled onto their pedestals, she once more moved to stand beside Gerry. "Now we'll walk down the line. You make each do a sit-up before we send them out."

One by one the cats rose on their haunches and pawed the air. Jo and Gerry moved down their ranks. The heat was becoming oppressive, and Jo shifted her shoulders, longing for a cool shower and a change of clothes. When they came to Hamlet, he ignored the command with a rebellious snarl.

Bad-tempered brute, thought Jo absently as she waited for Gerry to reissue the command. He did so but moved forward as if to emphasize the words.

"No, not so close!" Jo warned quickly. Even as she spoke, she saw the change in Hamlet's eyes.

Instinctively, she stepped over, nudging Gerry back and shielding his body with hers. Hamlet struck out, claws extended. There was a moment of blind heat in her shoulder as the skin ripped. Swiftly, she was facing the cat, holding tightly onto Gerry's arm as they stood just out of range.

"Don't run," she ordered, feeling his jerk of panic. Her arm was on fire as the blood began to flow freely. Keeping her movements quick but smooth, she took the whip from Gerry's nerveless hand and cracked it hard, using her left arm.

She knew that if Hamlet continued his defiance and attacked, it was hopeless. The other cats were certain to join in a melee. It would be over before anything could be done. Already, Abra shifted restlessly and bared her teeth.

"Open the chute," Jo called out. Her voice was cool as ice. "Back toward the safety cage," she instructed Gerry as she gave the cats their signal to leave the arena. "I've got to get them out one at a time. Move slow, and if I tell you to stop, you stop dead. Understand?"

She heard him swallow as she watched the cats begin to leap off their pedestals and file into the chute. "He got you. Is it bad?" The words were barely a whisper and drenched in terror.

"I said go." Half the cats were gone, and still Hamlet's eyes were locked on hers. There was no time to waste. One part of her brain heard shouting outside the cage, but she blocked it out and focused all her concentration on the cat. "Go now," she repeated to Gerry. "Do as you're told."

He swallowed again and began to back away. Long seconds dragged until she heard the rattle of the safety cage door. When his turn came, Hamlet made no move to leave his seat. Jo was alone with him. She could smell the heat, the scent of the wild and the fragrance of her own blood. Her arm was alive with pain. Slowly, she tested him by backing up. The safety cage seemed hundreds of miles away. The cat tensed immediately, and she stopped. She knew he would not let her cross the arena. Outrunning him was impossible, as the distance between them could be covered in one spring. She had to outbluff him instead.

"Out," she ordered firmly. "Out, Hamlet." As he continued to watch her, Jo felt a trickle of sweat slide down between her shoulder blades. Her skin was clammy with it in contrast to the warmth of the blood that ran down her arm. There was a sudden, vivid picture inside her head of her father being dragged around the cage. Fear tripped inside her throat. There was a lightness fluttering in the top of her head, and she knew that a moment's terror would cause her to faint. She stiffened her spine and pushed it away.

Speed was important. The longer she allowed the cat to remain in the arena after his cue, the more defiant he would become. And the more dangerous. As yet he was unaware that he held her at such a sharp disadvantage. "Out, Hamlet." Jo repeated the command with a crack of the whip. He leaped from the pedestal. Jo's stomach trembled. She locked every muscle, and as the cat hesitated, she repeated the command. He was confused, and she knew this could work as an advantage or a curse. Confused, he might spring or retreat. Her fingers tightened on the stock of the whip and trembled. The cat paced nervously and watched her.

"Hamlet!" She raised her voice and bit off each syllable. "Go out." To the words she added the hand signal she had used before he was fully trained to voice command.

As if rebuffed, Hamlet relaxed his tail and padded into the chute. Before the door slid completely closed, Jo sank to her knees. Her body began to quake fiercely with the aftershock. No more than five minutes had passed since Hamlet had defied Gerry's command, but her muscles bore the strain of hours. For an instant her vision blurred. Even as she shook her head to clear it, Keane was on the ground beside her.

She heard him swear, ripping the tattered sleeve of her blouse from her arm. He fired questions at her, but she could do no more than shake her head and gulp in air. Focusing on him, she noticed his eyes were unusually dark against his face.

"What?" She followed his voice but not the words. He swore again, sharply enough to penetrate the first layer of her shock. He pulled her to her feet, then continuing the motion smoothly, lifted her into his arms. "Don't." Her mind struggled to break through the fog and function. "I'm all right."

"Shut up," he said harshly as he carried her from the cage. "Just shut up."

Because speaking cost her some effort, Jo obeyed. Closing her eyes, she let the mixture of excited voices whirl around her. Her arm screamed with pain, but the throbbing reassured her. Numbness would have terrified her. Still she kept her eyes shut, not yet having the courage to look at the damage. Being alive was enough.

When she opened her eyes again, Keane was carrying her into the administration wagon. At the sound of the chaos that followed them, Duffy strode through from his office. "What the..." he began, then stopped and paled beneath his freckles. He moved quickly forward as Keane set Jo in a chair. "How bad?"

"I don't know yet," Keane muttered. "Get a towel and the first-aid kit."

Buck had come in behind them and, already having secured the items, handed them to Keane. Then he moved to a cabinet and located a bottle of brandy.

"It's not too bad," Jo managed. Because her voice was tolerably steady, she screwed up her courage and looked down. Keane had fastened a rough bandage from the remains of her sleeve. Though the flow of blood had slowed, there were streaks of it down her arm, and too much spreading from the wound to be certain how extensive the cuts were. Nausea rocked in her stomach.

"How do you know?" Keane demanded between his teeth as he began to clean the wound. He wrung out the towel in the basin Buck set beside him.

"It's not bleeding that badly." Jo swallowed the queasiness. As her mind began to clear, she frowned at the tone of Keane's voice. Feeling her stare, he glanced up. In his eyes was such fury, she pulled away.

"Be still," he ordered roughly and gave his attention back to her arm.

The cat had delivered only a glancing blow, but even so, there were four long slices in her upper arm. Jo set her jaw as pain ripped through her. Keane's brusqueness brought more hurt, and she fought to show no reaction to either. The aftermath of fear was bubbling through her. She longed to be held, to be soothed by the hands that tended to her wound.

"She's going to need stitches," Keane said without looking at her.

"And an antitoxin shot," Buck added, handing Jo a generous glass of brandy. "Drink this, honey. It'll help settle you."

The gentleness in his voice nearly undid her. He laid his big hand against her cheek, and for a moment she pressed against it.

"Drink now," Buck ordered again. Obediently, Jo lifted the glass and swallowed. The room whirled, then snapped into focus. She made a small sound and pressed the glass to her forehead. "Tell me what happened in there." Buck crouched down beside her as Keane began to apply a temporary bandage.

Jo took a moment to draw air in and out of her lungs. She lowered the glass and spoke steadily. "Hamlet didn't respond, and Gerry repeated a command, but he stepped forward. Too close. I saw Hamlet's eyes, and I knew. I should have moved faster. I should have been watching him more carefully. It was a stupid mistake." She stared into the brandy as she berated herself.

"She stepped between the boy and the cat." Keane bit off the words as he completed the bandaging. Rising, he moved to the brandy and poured. Not once did he turn to look at Jo. Hurt, she stared at his back before looking back at Buck.

"How's Gerry?"

Buck urged the glass back to her lips. A faint tint of pink was creeping into her cheeks. "Pete's with him. Got his head between his knees. He'll be fine."

Jo nodded. "I guess I'll have to go to town and have this seen to." She handed the glass to Buck and wondered if she dare attempt to rise yet. With another deep breath, she glanced at Duffy. "Make sure he's ready to go in when I get back."

Keane turned from the window. "Go in where?" His face was set in hard lines.

In response, Jo's voice was chilled. "In the cage." She turned her eyes to Buck. "We should be able to have a short run-through before the evening show."

"No." Jo's head snapped up as Keane spoke. For a long moment they stared at each other with odd, unreasonable antagonism. "You're not going back in there today." His voice held curt authority.

"Of course I am," Jo countered, managing to keep the combination of pain and anger from her words. "And if Gerry wants to be a cat man, he's going in, too."

"Jo's right," Buck put in, trying to soothe what he sensed was an explosive situation. "It's like falling off a horse. You can't wait too long before you get back up, or you won't ride again."

Keane never took his eyes from Jo. He continued as if Buck hadn't spoken. "I won't permit it."

"You can't stop me." Indignation forced her to her feet. The brisk movement caused her arm to protest, and her struggle against it showed momentarily in her eyes.

"Yes, I can." Keane took a long swallow of brandy. "I own this circus."

Jo's fists tightened at his tone, at his careless use of his authority. Not once since he had knelt beside her in the cage had he given her any sign of comfort or reassurance. She had needed it from him. To masquerade its trembling, she kept her voice low. "But you don't own me, Mr. Prescott. And if you'll check your papers and the legalities, you'll see you don't own the lions or my equipment. I bought them, and I maintain

them out of my salary. My contract doesn't give
you the right to tell me when I can or can't rehearse my cats."

Keane's face was granite hard. "Neither does
it give you the right to set up in the Big Top without my permission."

"Then I'll set up some place else," she tossed
back. "But I *will* set up. That cat will be worked
again today. I won't take the risk of losing
months of training."

"But you will risk being killed," Keane shot
back and slammed down his glass.

"What do you care?" Jo shouted. All control
deserted her. The cuts were deep on her emotions as well as her flesh. She had passed through
a terror more acute than she had known since the
night of her parents' death. More than anything
else, she wanted to feel Keane's arms around her.
She wanted to know the security she had felt
when he had let her weep out her grief for Ari in
his arms. "I'm nothing to you!" Her head shook
quickly, tossing her hair. There was a bubble of
hysteria in her voice, and Buck reached out to lay
a hand on her shoulder.

"Jo," he warned in his soft, rumbling voice.

"No!" She shook her head and spoke rapidly.
"He hasn't the right. You haven't the right to in-
terfere with my life." She flared at Keane again
with eyes vivid with emotion. "I know what I
have to do. I know what I *will* do. Why should it

matter to you? You aren't legally responsible if I get mauled. No one's going to sue you."

"Hold on, Jo." This time Buck spoke firmly. As he took her uninjured arm, he felt the tremors shooting through her. "She's too upset to know what she's saying," he told Keane.

There was a mask over Keane's face which concealed all emotion. "Oh, I think she knows what she's saying," he disagreed quietly. For a moment there was only the sound of Jo shuddering and the splash of brandy being poured into a glass. "You do what you have to do, Jo," he said after drinking again. "You're perfectly correct that I haven't any rights where you're concerned. Take her into town," he told Buck, then turned back to the window.

"Come on, Jo." Buck urged her to the door, slipping a supportive arm around her waist. Even as they stepped outside, Rose came running from the direction of the midway.

"Jo!" Her face was white with concern. "Jo, I just heard." She glanced at the bandage with wide, terrified eyes. "How bad is it?"

"Just scratches, really," Jo assured her. She added the best smile she could muster. "Buck's going to take me into town for a couple of stitches."

"Are you sure?" She looked up at the tall man for reassurance. "Buck?"

"Several stitches," he corrected but patted Rose's hand. "But it's not too bad."

"Do you want me to come with you?" She fell into step beside them as Buck began to lead Jo again.

"No. Thank you, Rose." Jo smiled with more feeling. "I'll be fine."

Because of the smile, Rose was able to relax. "I thought when I heard...well, I imagined all sorts of terrible things. I'm glad you're not badly hurt." They had reached Buck's truck, and Rose leaned over to kiss Jo's cheek. "We all love you so."

"I know." Squeezing her hand, Jo let Buck help her into the cab of his truck. As he maneuvered from the lot, Jo rested her head against the back of the seat and shut her eyes. Never could she remember feeling more spent, more battered.

"Hurt bad?" Buck asked as they switched to an asphalt road.

"Yes," she answered simply, thinking of her heart as much as her arm.

"You'll feel better when you're patched up."

Jo kept her eyes shut, knowing some wounds never heal. Or if they did, they left scars that ached at unexpected times.

"You shouldn't have gone off on him that way, Jo." There was light censure in Buck's voice.

"He shouldn't have interfered," Jo retorted. "It's none of his business. *I'm* none of his business."

"Jo, it's not like you to be so hard."

"Hard?" She opened her eyes and turned to Buck. "What about him? Couldn't he have been kinder, shown even the barest trace of compassion? Did he have to speak to me as if I were a criminal?"

"Jo, the man was terrified. You're only looking at this from one side." He scratched his beard and gave a gusty sigh. "You can't know what it's like to be outside that cage, helpless when someone you care about is facing down death. I had to all but knock him unconscious to keep him out of there until we got it through his head that he'd just get you killed for sure. He was scared, Jo. We were all scared."

Jo shook her head, certain Buck exaggerated because of his affection for her. Keane's voice had been hard, his eyes angry. "He doesn't care," she corrected quietly. "Not like the rest of you. You didn't swear at me. You weren't cold."

"Jo, people have different ways—" Buck began, but she interrupted.

"I know he wouldn't want to see me hurt, Buck. He's not heartless or cruel." She sighed as all the force of anger and fear washed out of her body and left her empty. "Please, I don't want to talk about him."

Buck heard the weariness in her voice and patted her hand. "Okay, honey, just relax. We'll have you all fixed up in no time."

Not all fixed up, Jo thought. Far from all fixed up.

Chapter Eleven

As the weeks passed, Jo's arm lost its stiffness. She healed cleanly. The only traces were thin scars that promised to fade but not disappear. She found, however, that some spark had gone out of her life. Constantly, she fought against a vague dissatisfaction. Nothing—not her work, not her friends, not her books—brought about the contentment she had grown up with. She had become a woman, and her needs had shifted. Jo knew the root of her problem was Keane, but the knowledge was not a solution. He had left the circus again on the very night of her accident. Nearly four weeks later he had not returned.

Three times Jo had sat down to write him, needing to assuage her guilt for the harsh things she had said to him. Three times she had torn up the paper in frustration. No matter how she re-arranged the words, they were wrong. Instead, she clung to the hope that he would come back one last time. If, she felt, they could part as friends, without bitterness or hard words, she could accept the separation. Willing this to happen, she was able to return to her routine with some tranquility. She rehearsed, performed, joined in the daily duties of circus life. She waited. The caravan moved closer to Chicago.

Jo stood in the steaming Big Top on a late August afternoon. Dressed in a leotard, she worked on ground exercises with the Beirot Brothers. It was this daily regimentation that had aided in keeping her arm limber. She could now move into a back walk-over without feeling any protest in her injured arm.

"I feel good," Jo told Raoul as they worked out. "I feel really good." She did a quick series of pirouettes.

"You don't keep your shoulder in shape by dancing on your feet," Raoul challenged.

"My shoulder's fine," she tossed back, then proved her point by bending into a handstand. Slowly, she lowered her legs to a forty-five degree angle, bringing one foot to rest on the knee of the opposite leg. "It's perfect." She executed a forward roll and sprang to her feet. "I'm strong as an ox," she claimed and did a quick back handspring followed by a back flip.

She landed at Keane's feet.

The cascade of emotions that raced through her reflected briefly in her eyes before she regained her balance. "I didn't—I didn't know you were back." Instantly, she regretted the inanity of the words but could find no others. The longing was raw in her to hurl herself into his arms. She wondered that he could not feel her need through the pores of her skin.

"I just got in." His eyes continued to search her face after his hands dropped to his sides. "This is my mother," he added. "Rachael Loring, Jovilette Wilder."

At his words, Jo's gaze moved from his face. She saw the woman beside him. If she had seen Rachael Loring in a crowd of two thousand, she would have known her for Keane's mother. The bone structure was the same, though hers was more elegant. Her brows were golden wings, flaring out at the end, as Keane's did. Her hair was smooth, brushed up and away from her face with no gray to mar its tawny perfection. But it was the eyes that sent a jolt through Jo. She had not thought to see them in anyone's face but Keane's. The woman was dressed simply in an unpretentiously tailored suit that bespoke taste and wealth. There was, however, none of the cool, distant polish that Jo had always attributed to the woman who had taken her son and left Frank. There was a charm to the smile that curved in greeting.

"Jovilette, such a lovely name. Keane's told me of you." She extended her hand, and Jo accepted, intending a quick, impersonal shake. Rachael Loring, however, laid her other hand atop their joined ones and added warmth. "Keane tells me you were very close to Frank. Perhaps we could talk."

The affection in her voice confused Jo into a stumbling reply. "I—Yes. I—if you'd like."

"I should like very much." She squeezed Jo's hand again before releasing it. "Perhaps you have time to show me around?" She smiled with the question, and Jo found it increasingly difficult to remain aloof. "I'm sure there've been some changes since I was here last. You must have some business to attend to," she said, looking up at Keane. "I'm sure Jovilette will take good care of me. Won't you, dear?" Without waiting for either to respond, Rachael tucked her arm through Jo's and began to walk. "I knew your parents," she said as Keane watched them move away. "Not terribly well, I'm afraid. They came here the same year I left. But I recall they were both thrilling performers. Keane tells me you've followed your father's profession."

"Yes, I..." She hesitated, feeling oddly at a disadvantage. "I did," she finished lamely.

"You're so young." Rachael gave her a gentle smile. "How terribly brave you must be."

"No...no, not really. It's my job."

"Yes, of course." Rachael laughed at some private memory. "I've heard that before."

They were outside now, and she paused to look thoughtfully around her. "I think perhaps I was wrong. It hasn't really changed, not in thirty years. It's a wonderful place, isn't it?"

"Why did you leave?" As soon as the words were spoken, Jo regretted them. "I'm sorry," she said quickly. "I shouldn't have asked."

"Of course you should." Rachael sighed and patted Jo's hand. "It's only natural. Duffy's still here, Keane tells me." At the change in subject, Jo imagined her question had been evaded.

"Yes, I suppose he always will be."

"Could we have some coffee, or some tea, perhaps?" Rachael smiled again. "It's such a long drive from town. Is your trailer nearby?"

"It's just over in the back yard."

"Oh, yes." Rachael laughed and began to walk again. "The neighborhood that never changes over thousands of miles. Do you know the story of the dog and the bones?" she asked. Though Jo knew it well, she said nothing. "One version is that a roustabout gave his dog a bone every night after dinner. The dog would bury the bone under the trailer, then the next day try to dig it back up. Of course, it was fifty miles behind in an empty lot. He never figured it out." Quietly, she laughed to herself.

Feeling awkward, Jo opened the door to her trailer. How could this woman be the one she had resented all of her life? How could this be the cold, heartless woman who had left Frank? Oddly, Rachael seemed totally at ease in the narrow confines of the trailer.

"How efficient these are." She looked around with interest and approval. "You must barely re-

alize you're on wheels.'' Casually, she picked up
the volume of Thoreau which lay on Jo's counter.
"Keane told me you have an avid interest in lit-
erature. In language, too,'' she added, glancing
up from the book. Her eyes were golden and direct like her son's. Jo was tossed back suddenly
to the first morning of the season when she had
looked down and found Keane's eyes on her.

It made her uncomfortable to learn Keane had
discussed her with his mother. "I have some tea,''
Jo told her as she moved toward the kitchen.
"It's a better gamble than my coffee.''

"That's fine,'' Rachael said agreeably and
followed her. "I'll just sit here while you fix it.''
She settled herself with apparent ease at the tiny
table across from the kitchen.

"I'm afraid I haven't anything else to offer
you.'' Jo kept her back turned as she routed
through her cupboard.

"Tea and conversation,'' Rachael answered in
mild tones, "will be fine.''

Jo sighed and turned. "I'm sorry.'' She shook
her head. "I'm being rude. I just don't know
what to say to you, Mrs. Loring. I've resented
you for as long as I can remember. Now you're
here and not at all as I imagined.'' She managed
to smile, albeit ruefully. "You're not cold and
hateful, and you look so much like...'' She
stopped, horrified that she had nearly blurted out
Keane's name. For a moment her eyes were utterly naked.

Rachael smoothed over the awkwardness. "I don't wonder you resented me if you were as close to Frank as Keane tells me. Jovilette," she said softly, "did Frank resent me, too?"

Helpless, Jo responded to the hint of sadness. "No. Not while I knew him. I don't think Frank was capable of resentments."

"You understood him well, didn't you?" Rachael watched as Jo poured boiling water into mugs. "I understood him, too," she continued as Jo brought the mugs to the table. "He was a dreamer, a marvelous free spirit." Absently, she stirred her tea.

Consumed with curiosity, Jo sat across from her and waited for the story she sensed was coming.

"I was eighteen when I met him. I had come to the circus with a cousin. The Colossus was a bit smaller in those days," she added with a reminiscent smile, "but it was all the same. Oh, the magic!" She shook her head and sighed. "We tumbled into love so fast, married against all my family's objections and went on the road. It was exciting. I learned the web routine and helped out in wardrobe."

Jo's eyes widened. "You performed?"

"Oh, yes." Rachael's cheeks tinted a bit with pride. "I was quite good. Then I became pregnant. We were both like children waiting for Christmas. I wasn't quite nineteen when I had Keane, and I'd been with the circus for nearly a year. Things became difficult over the next season. I was young and a bit frightened of Keane. I panicked if he sneezed and was constantly dragging Frank into town to see doctors. How patient he was.''

Rachael leaned forward and took Jo's hand. ''Can you understand how hard this life is for one not meant for it? Can you see that through the magic of it, the excitement and wonder, there are hardships and fears and impossible demands? I was little more than a child myself, with an infant to care for, without the endurance or vocation of a trouper, without the experience or confidence of a mother. I lived on nerves for an entire season.'' She let out a little rush of breath. ''When it was over, I went home to Chicago.''

For the first time, Jo imagined the flight from Rachael's point of view. She could see a girl, younger than herself, in a strange, demanding world with a baby to care for. Over the years Jo had seen scores of people try the life she'd led and last only weeks. Still she shook her head in confusion.

''I think I understand how difficult it must have been for you. But if you and Frank loved each other, couldn't you have worked it out somehow?''

''How?'' Rachael countered. ''Should I have taken a house somewhere and lived with him half a year? I would have hated him. Should he have given up his life here and settled down with me and Keane? It would have destroyed everything I loved about him." Rachael shook her head, giving Jo a soft smile. "We did love each other, Jovilette, but not enough. Compromise isn't always possible, and neither of us were capable of adjusting to the needs of the other. I tried, and Frank would have tried had I asked him. But it was lost before it had really begun. We did the wisest thing under the circumstances." Looking into Jo's eyes, she saw youth and confidence. "It seems cold and hard to you, but it was no use dragging out a painful situation. He gave me Keane and two years I've always treasured. I gave him his freedom without bitterness. Ten years after Frank, I found happiness again." She smiled softly with the memory. "I loved Frank, and that love remains as young and sweet as the day I met him."

Jo swallowed. She searched for some way to apologize for a grudge held for a lifetime. "He—Frank kept a scrapbook on Keane. He followed the Chicago papers."

"Did he?" Rachael beamed, then leaned back in her chair and lifted her mug. "How like him. Was he happy, Jovilette? Did he have what he wanted?"

"Yes," Jo answered without hesitation. "Did you?"

Rachael's eyes came back to Jo's. For a moment the look was speculative, then it grew warm. "What a good heart you have, generous and understanding. Yes, I had what I wanted. And you, Jovilette, what do you want?"

At ease now, Jo shook her head and smiled. "More than I can have."

"You're too smart for that," Rachael observed, studying her. "I think you're a fighter, not a dreamer. When the time comes to make your choice, you won't settle for anything less than all." She smiled at Jo's intent look, then rose. "Will you show me your lions? I can't tell you how I'm looking forward to seeing you perform."

"Yes, of course." Jo stood, then hesitated. She held out her hand. "I'm glad you came."

Rachael accepted the gesture. "So am I."

Throughout the rest of the day Jo looked for Keane without success. After meeting and talking with his mother, it had become even more imperative that she speak with him. Her conscience would have no rest until she made amends. By showtime she had not yet found him.

Each act seemed to run on and on as she fretted for the finish. He would be with his mother in the audience, and undoubtedly she would find him after the show. She strained with impatience as the acts dragged.

After the finale she stood at the back door, unsure whether to wait or to go to his trailer. She was struck with both relief and alarm when she saw him approaching.

"Jovilette." Rachael spoke first, taking Jo's hands in hers. "How marvelous you were, and how stunning. I see why Keane said you had an untamed beauty."

Surprised, Jo glanced up at Keane but met impassive amber eyes. "I'm glad you enjoyed it."

"Oh, I can't tell you how much. The day has brought me some very precious memories. Our talk this afternoon meant a great deal to me." To Jo's surprise, Rachael leaned over and kissed her. "I hope to see you again. I'm going to say goodbye to Duffy before you drive me back, Keane," she continued. "I'll meet you in the car. Goodbye, Jovilette."

"Goodbye, Mrs. Loring." Jo watched her go before she turned to Keane. "She's a wonderful person. She makes me ashamed."

"There's no need for that." He tucked his hands into his pockets and watched her. "We both had our reasons for resentments, and we were both wrong. How's your arm?"

"Oh." Jo's fingers traveled to the wound automatically. "It's fine. There's barely any scarring."

"Good." The word was short and followed by silence. For a moment Jo felt her courage fail her.

"Keane," she began, then forced herself to meet his eyes directly. "I want to apologize for the horrible way I behaved after the accident."

"I told you once before," he said coolly, "I don't care for apologies."

"Please." Jo swallowed her pride and touched his arm. "I've been saving this one for a very long time. I didn't mean those things I said," she added quickly. "I hope you'll forgive me." It wasn't the eloquent apology she had planned, but it was all she could manage. His expression never altered.

"There's nothing to forgive."

"Keane, please." Jo grabbed his arm again as he turned to go. "Don't leave me feeling as if you don't forgive me. I know I said dreadful things. You have every right to be furious, but couldn't you—can't we be friends again?"

Something flickered over his face. Lifting his hand, he touched the back of it to her cheek. "You have a habit of disconcerting me, Jovilette." He dropped his hand, then thrust it into his pocket. "I've left something for you with Duffy. Be happy." He walked away from her while she dealt with the finality of his tone. He was walking out of her life. She watched him until he disappeared.

Jo had thought she would feel something, but there was nothing; no pain, no tears, no desperation. She had not known a human being could be so empty and still live.

"Jo." Duffy lumbered up to her, then held out a thick envelope. "Keane left this for you." Then he moved past her, anxious to see that all straggling towners were nudged on their way.

Jo felt all emotions had been stripped away. Absently, she glanced at the envelope as she walked to her trailer. Without enthusiasm, she stepped inside, then tore it open. She remained standing as she pulled out the contents. It took her several moments to decipher the legal jargon. She read the group of papers through twice before sitting down.

He's given it to me, she thought. Still she could not comprehend the magnitude of it. *He's given me the circus.*

Chapter Twelve

O'Hare Airport was an army of people and a cacophony of sound. Nearly losing herself in the chaos of it, Jo struggled through the masses and competed for a cab. At first she had merely gawked at the snow like a towner seeing his first sword swallower. Then, though she shivered inside the corduroy coat she had bought for the trip, she began to enjoy it. It was beautiful as it lay over the city, and it helped to turn her mind from the purpose of her journey. Never had she been north so late in the year. Chicago in November was a sensational sight.

She had learned, after the initial shock had worn off, that Keane had not only given her the circus but a responsibility as well. Almost immediately there had been contracts to negotiate. She had been tossed into a sea of paperwork, forced to rely heavily on Duffy's experience as she tried to regain her balance. As the season had come to a close, Jo had attempted a dozen times to call Chicago. Each time, she had hung up before Keane's number could be dialed. It would be, she had decided, more appropriate to see him

in person. Her trip had been postponed a few
weeks due to Jamie and Rose's wedding.

It was there, as she had stood as maid of
honor, that Jo had realized what she must do.
There was only one thing she truly wanted, and
that was to be with Keane. Watching Rose's face
as their vows had been exchanged, Jo had recalled her unflagging determination to win the
man she loved.

And will I stay here? Jo had demanded of herself thousands of miles away from him. No. Her
heart had begun to thud as she had mapped out
a plan. She would go to Chicago to see him. She
would not be turned away. He had wanted her
once; she would make him want her again. She
would not live out her life without at least some
small portion of it being part of his. He didn't
have to love her. It was enough that she loved
him.

And so, shivering against the unfamiliar cold,
Jo scrambled into a cab and headed across town.
She brushed her hair free of snow with chilled
fingers, thinking how idiotic she had been to forget to buy a hat and gloves. What if he isn't
home? she thought suddenly. What if he's gone
to Europe or Japan or California? Panic made
her giddy, and she pushed it down. He has to be
home. It's Sunday, and he's sitting at home
reading or going over a brief—or entertaining a
woman, she thought, appalled. I should stop and
call. I should tell the driver to take me back to the

airport. Closing her eyes, Jo fought to regain her calm. She took long, deep breaths and stared at the buildings and sidewalks. Gradually, she felt the tiny gurgle of hysteria dissipate.

I won't be afraid, she told herself and tried to believe it. I won't be afraid. But Jovilette, the woman who reclined on a living rug of lions, was very much afraid. What if he rejected her? I won't let him reject me, she told herself with a confident lift of her chin. *I'll seduce him.* She pressed her fingers to her temples. *I wouldn't know how to begin.* I've got to tell the driver to turn around.

But before she could form the words, the cab pulled up to a curb. With the precision of a robot, Jo paid the fare, overtipping in her agitation, and climbed out.

Long after the cab had pulled away, she stood staring up at the massive glass-girdled building. Snow waltzed around her, sprinkling her hair and shoulders. A jostle from a rushing pedestrian broke the spell. She picked up her suitcases and hurried through the front door of the apartment buildings.

The lobby was enormous, with smoked glass walls and a deep shag carpet. Not knowing she should give her name at the desk, Jo wandered toward the elevators, innocently avoiding detection by merging with a group of tenants. Once inside the car, Jo pushed the button for the penthouse with a nerveless forefinger. The chatter of those in the elevator with her registered only as a distant humming. She never noticed when the car stopped for their departure.

When it stopped a second time and the doors slid open, she stared at the empty space for ten full seconds. Only as the automatic doors began to close did she snap out of her daze. Pushing them open again, she stepped through and into the hall. Her legs were wobbly, but she forced them to move forward in the direction of the penthouse. Panic sped up and down her spine until she set down her bags and leaned her brow against Keane's door. She urged air in and out of her lungs. She remembered that Rachael Loring had called her a fighter. Jo swallowed, lifted her chin and knocked. The wait was mercifully brief before Keane opened the door. She saw surprise light his eyes as he stared at her.

Her hair was dusted with snow as it lay over the shoulders of her coat. Her face glowed with the cold, and her eyes were bright, nearly feverish with her struggle for calm. Only once did her mouth tremble before she spoke.

"Hello, Keane."

He only stared, his eyes running over her in disbelief. He was leaner, she thought as she studied his face. As she filled herself with the sight of him, she saw he wore a sweatshirt and jeans. His feet were bare. He hadn't shaved, and her hand itched to test the roughness of his beard.

"What are you doing here?" Jo felt a resurgence of panic. His tone was harsh, and he had not answered her smile. She strained for poise.

"May I come in?" she asked, her smile cracking.

"What?" He seemed distracted by the question. His brows lowered into a frown.

"May I come in?" she repeated, barely defeating the urge to turn tail and run.

"Oh, yes, of course. I'm sorry." Running a hand through his hair, Keane stepped back and gestured her inside.

Instantly, Jo's shoes sank into the luxurious pile of the buff-colored carpet. For a moment she allowed herself to gaze around the room, using the time for the additional purpose of regaining her composure. It was an open, sweeping room with sharp, contrasting colors. There was a deep brown sectional sofa with a chrome and glass coffee table. There were high-backed chairs in soft creams and vivid slashes of blue in chunky floor pillows. There were paintings, one she thought she recognized as a Picasso, and a sculpture she was certain was a Rodin.

On the far right of the room there was an elevation of two steps. Just beyond was a huge expanse of glass that featured a spreading view of Chicago. Jo moved toward it with undisguised curiosity. Now, unexplicably, fear had lessened. She found that once she had stepped over the threshold she had committed herself. She was no longer afraid.

"It's wonderful," she said, turning back to him. "How marvelous to have a whole city at your feet every day. You must feel like a king."

"I've never thought of it that way." With half the room between them, he studied her. She looked small and fragile with the bustling city at her back.

"I would," she said, and now her smile came easily. "I'd stand at the window and feel regal and pompous."

At last she saw his lips soften and curve. "Jovilette," he said quietly. "What are you doing in my world?"

"I needed to talk to you," she answered simply. "I had to come here to do it."

He moved to her then, but slowly, with his eyes on hers. "It must be important."

"I thought so."

His brow lifted, then he shrugged. "Well, then, we'll talk. But first, let's have your coat."

Jo's cold fingers fumbled with the buttons and caused Keane to frown again. "Good heavens, you're frozen." He captured her hands between his and swore. "Where are your gloves?" he demanded like an irate parent. "It must be all of twelve degrees outside."

"I forgot to buy any," Jo told him as she dealt with the heavenly feeling of his hands restoring warmth to hers.

"Idiot. Don't you know better than to come to Chicago in November without gloves?"

"No." Jo responded to his anger with a cheerful smile. "I've never been to Chicago in November before. It's wonderful."

His eyes lifted from her hands to her face. He watched her for a long moment, then she heard him sigh. "I'd nearly convinced myself I could be cured."

Jo's eyes clouded with concern. "Have you been ill?"

Keane laughed with a shake of his head, then he pushed away the question and became brisk again. "Here, let's have your coat. I'll get you some coffee."

"You needn't bother," she began as he undid the buttons on the coat himself and drew it from her shoulders.

"I'd feel better if I was certain your circulation was restored." He paused and looked down at her as he laid her coat over his arm. She wore a green angora sweater with pearl buttons and a gray skirt in thin wool. The soft fabric draped softly at her breasts and over her hips and thighs. Her shoes were dainty and impractical sling-back heels.

"Is something wrong?"

"I've never seen you wear anything but a costume or jeans."

"Oh." Jo laughed and combed her fingers through her damp hair. "I expect I look different."

"Yes, you do." His voice was low, and there was a frown in his eyes. "Right now you look as if you've come from college for the holidays." He touched the ends of her hair, then turned away. "Sit down. I'll get the coffee."

A bit puzzled by his mercurial moods, Jo wandered about the room, finally ignoring a chair to kneel beside one of the pillows near the picture window. Though the carpet swallowed Keane's footsteps, she sensed his return.

"How wonderful to have a real winter, if just for the snow." She turned a radiant face his way. "I've always wondered what Christmas is like with snow and icicles." Images of snowflakes danced in her eyes. Seeing he carried two mugs of coffee, she rose and took one. "Thank you."

"Are you warm enough?" he asked after a moment.

Jo nodded and sat in one of the two chairs opposite the sofa. The novelty of the city made her mission seem like a grand adventure. Keane sat beside her, and for a moment they drank in companionable silence.

"What did you want to talk to me about, Jo?"

Jo swallowed, ignoring the faint trembling in her chest. "A couple of things. The circus, for one." She shifted in her chair until she faced him. "I didn't write because I felt it too important. I didn't phone for the same reason. Keane . . ." All her carefully thought-out speeches deserted her. "You can't just give something like that away. I can't take it from you."

"Why not?" He shrugged and sipped his coffee. "We both know it's always been yours. A piece of paper doesn't change that one way or the other."

"Keane, Frank left it to you."

"And I gave it to you."

Jo made a small sound of frustration. "Perhaps if I could pay you for it . . ."

"Someone asked me once what was the value of a dream or the price of a human spirit." Jo shifted her eyes to his helplessly. "I didn't have an answer then. Do you have one now?"

She sighed and shook her head. "I don't know what to say to you. 'Thank you' is far from adequate."

"It's not necessary, either," Keane told her. "I simply gave back what was yours in any case. What else was there, Jo? You said there were a couple of things."

This was it, Jo's brain told her. Carefully, she set down the coffee and rose. Waiting for her stomach to settle, she walked a few feet out into the room, then turned. She allowed herself a deep breath before she met Keane's eyes.

"I want to be your mistress," she said with absolute calm.

"What?" Both Keane's face and voice registered utter shock.

Jo swallowed and repeated. "I want to be your mistress. That's still the right term, isn't it, or is it antiquated? Is *lover* right? I've never done this before."

Slowly, Keane set his mug beside hers and rose. He did not move toward her but watched her with probing eyes. "Jo, you don't know what you're saying."

"Oh, yes, I do," she cut him off and nodded. "I might not have the terminology exactly right, but I do know what I mean, and I'm sure you do, too. I want to be with you," she continued and took a step toward him. "I want you to make love to me. I want to live with you if you'll let me, or at least close by."

"Jo, you're not talking sensibly." Sharply, Keane broke into her speech. Turning away, he thrusted his hands into his pockets and balled them into fists. "You don't know what you're asking."

"Don't I appeal to you anymore?"

Keane whirled, infuriated with the trace of curiosity in her voice. "How can you ask me that?" he demanded. "Of course you appeal to me! I'm not dead or in the throes of senility!"

She moved closer to him. "Then if I want you, and you want me, why can't we be lovers?"

Keane swore violently and grabbed her shoulders. "Do you think I could have you for a win-

ter and then blithely let you go? Do you think I
could untangle myself at the start of the season
and watch you stroll out of my life? Haven't you
the sense to see what you do to me?" He shook
her hard with the question, stealing any breath
she might have used to answer him.

"You make me crazy!" Abruptly, he dragged
her against him. His mouth bruised hers, his fingers dug into her flesh. Jo's head spun with confusion and pain and ecstasy. It seemed centuries
since she had tasted his mouth on hers. She heard
him groan as he tore himself away. He turned,
leaving her to find her own balance as the room
swayed. "What do I have to do to be rid of
you?" His words came in furious undertones.

Jo blew out a breath. "I don't think kissing me
like that is a very good start."

"I'm aware of that," he murmured. She
watched the rise and fall of his shoulders. "I've
been trying to avoid doing it since I opened the
door."

Quietly, Jo walked to him and put a hand on
his arm. "You're tense," she discovered and automatically sought to soothe the muscles. "I'm
sorry if I'm going about this the wrong way. I
thought telling you outright would be better than
trying to seduce you. I don't think I'd be very
good at that."

Keane made a sound somewhere between a
laugh and a moan. "Jovilette," he murmured
before he turned and gathered her into his arms.

"How do I resist you? How many times must I pull away before I'm free of you? Even the thought of you drives me mad."

"Keane." She sighed and shut her eyes. "I've wanted you to hold me for so long. I want to belong to you, even for just a little while."

"No." He pulled away, then forced her chin up with his thumb and forefinger. "Don't you see that once would be too much and a lifetime wouldn't be enough? I love you too much to let you go and enough to know I have to." Shock robbed her of speech. She only stared as he continued. "It was different when I didn't know, when I thought I was—how did you put it? 'Dazzled.'" He smiled briefly at the word. "I was certain if I could make love to you, I could get you out of my system. Then, the night Ari died, I held you while you slept. I realized I was in love with you, had been in love with you right from the beginning."

"But you..." Jo shook her head as if to clear it. "You never told me, and you seemed so cold, so distant."

"I couldn't touch you without wanting more." He pulled her close again and for a moment buried his face in her hair. "But I couldn't stay away. I knew if I wanted to have you, to really have you, one of us had to give up what we did, what we were. I wondered if I could give up the law; it was really all I ever wanted to do. I discovered I wanted you more."

"Oh, Keane." She shook her head, but he put her from him suddenly.

"Then I found out that wouldn't work, either." Keane turned, paced to the window and stared out. The snow was falling heavily. "Every time you walked into that cage, I walked into hell. I thought perhaps I'd get used to it, but it only got worse. I tried leaving, coming back here, but I could never shake you loose. I kept coming back. The day you were hurt..." Keane paused. Jo heard him draw in his breath, and when he continued, his voice was deeper. "I watched you step in front of that boy and take the blow. I can't tell you what I felt at that moment; there aren't words for it. All I could think of was getting to you. I wonder if Pete ever told you that I decked him before Buck got to me. He took it very well, considering. Then I had to—to just stand there and watch while that cat stalked you. I've never known that kind of fear before. The kind that empties you out, body and soul."

He lapsed into silence. "Then it was over," he continued, "and I got to you. You were so white, and you were bleeding in my arms." He muttered an oath, then was silent again. He shook his head. "I wanted to burn the place down, get you away, strangle the cats with my bare hands. Anything. I wanted to hold you, but I couldn't get past the fear and the unreasonable anger at having been helpless. Before my hands stopped shaking, you were making plans to go back into that damnable cage. I wanted to kill you myself then and be done with it."

Slowly, Keane turned and walked back to her. "I saw it happen again every time I closed my eyes for weeks afterward. I can show you exactly where the scars are." He lifted a finger and traced four lines on her upper arm precisely where the claws had ripped her skin. He dropped his hand and shook his head. "I can't watch you go in the cage, Jo." He lifted his hand again and let it linger over her hair. "If I let you stay with me now, I wouldn't be able to let you go back to your own life. And I can't ask you to give it up."

"I wish you would." Solemn-eyed, Jo watched him. "I very much wish you would."

"Jo." Shaking his head, he turned away. "I know what it means to you."

"No more than the law means to you, I imagine," she said briskly. "But you said you were willing to give that up."

"Yes, but . . ."

"Oh, very well." She pushed back her hair. "If you won't ask me, I'll have to ask you. Will you marry me?"

Keane turned back, giving her his lowered brow frown. "Jo, you can't . . ."

"Of course I can. This is the twentieth century. If I want to ask you to marry me, then I will. I did," she pointed out.

"Jo, I don't . . ."

"Yes or no, please, counselor. This isn't an easy question." She stepped forward until they stood toe to toe. "I'm in love with you, and I want to marry you and have several babies. Is that agreeable?"

Keane's mouth opened and closed. He gave her an odd smile and lifted his hands to her shoulders. "This is rather sudden."

Jo felt a wild surge of joy. "Perhaps it is," she admitted. "I'll give you a minute to think about it. But I might as well tell you, I won't take no for an answer."

Keane's fingers traced the curve of her neck. "It seems I have little choice."

"None at all," she corrected. Boldly, she locked her arms around him and pulled his mouth down to hers. The kiss was instantly urgent, instantly searching. Joined, they lowered to the rug and clung. For a long, long moment, their lips were united in a language too complex for words. Then, as if to reassure himself she was real, Keane searched the familiar curves of her body, tasted the longed-for flavor of her skin.

"Why did I think I could live without you?" he whispered. His mouth came desperately back to hers. "Be sure, Jo, be sure." Roughened with emotion, his voice was low while the words were spoken against her lips. "I'll never be able to let you go. I'm asking you for everything."

"No. No, it's not like that. Hold me tighter. Kiss me again," she demanded as his lips roamed her face. "Kiss me." She wondered if the sound of pleasure she heard was his or her own. She had not known a kiss could be so intimate, so terrifyingly exciting. No, she thought as she soared with the knowledge that he loved her. He wasn't asking everything, he was giving it.

"I'm leaving something behind," she told him when their lips parted, "and replacing it with something infinitely more important." She buried her face in the curve of his neck. "When you realize how much I love you, you'll understand."

Keane drew away and stared down at her. At last he spoke, but it was only her name. It was a soft sigh of a sound. She smiled at it and lifted a hand to his cheek. "If there's a way to compromise . . ."

"No." She shook her head, remembering his mother's words. "Sometimes there can't be a compromise. We love each other enough not to need one. Please, don't think I'm making a sacrifice; I'm not." She smiled a little and rubbed her palm experimentally over the stubble of his neglected beard. "I don't regret one minute of my life in the circus, and I don't regret changing it. You've given me the circus, so I'll always be a part of it." Her smile faded, and her eyes grew serious. "Will you belong to me, Keane?"

He took her hand from his cheek and pressed it to his lips. "I already do. I love you, Jovilette. I'll spend a lifetime loving you."

"That's not long enough," she said as their lips met again. "I want more. I want forever."

With slow, building passion, his hands moved over her. Taking his time, he loosened the buttons on her sweater. "So beautiful," he murmured as his lips trailed down her throat and found the gentle swell. Jo's breath caught at the new intimacy. "You're trembling. I love knowing I can make your skin tremble under my hands." His lips roamed back to hers before he cradled her in his arms. "I've wanted to be with you, to hold you, just hold you, for so long. I can't remember not wanting it."

With a sigh washed with contentment, Jo snuggled against him. "Keane," she murmured.

"Hmm?"

"You never answered me."

"About what?" He kissed her closed lids, then tangled his fingers in her hair.

Jo opened her eyes. Her brows arched over them. "Are you going to marry me or not?"

Keane laughed, rolled her onto her back and planted a long, lingering kiss on her mouth. "Is tomorrow soon enough?"

* * * * *

COMING NEXT MONTH!

If you liked SECOND NATURE, there's good news in next month's shipment. In ONE SUMMER, Nora Roberts has given Lee's friend Bryan Mitchell her own story, in a romance that sizzles right across the entire country!

Having finished her work for Lee's magazine, photographer Bryan Mitchell moves on to her next assignment—to capture "An American Summer" on film. It's the job of a lifetime—especially as she'll be working and traveling with Shade Colby, a photographer whose work she admires. But she's not prepared for the strong clash of creative forces between them. They seem to disagree on just about everything. The battle of wills is on!

Yet, as their journey takes them from Los Angeles to Cape Cod, they both know they make the most beautiful pictures not separately, but together. Is it true that the camera never lies...? Find out next month in ONE SUMMER, so full of luscious images, it's a book that's worth a thousand pictures!

THE
LANGUAGE
of LOVE